She had to kiss Kno_____ these people?

"Quit looking like the instructor just issued a ____ sentence," he whispered through a brittle smile. "We're supposed to be married, remember?"

"Right," she said breathlessly.

"It's just a kiss," Knox said unsteadily. "We can handle it."

With anticipation and anxiety, Savannah's eyes fluttered shut as Knox's warm lips descended to hers. How many times had she dreamed of this? With a groan of pure delight she pressed herself against him. Their tongues played a game of hide-and-seek, and with every movement, Savannah grew more agitated, more needy. Knox tightened his hold on her, and she felt his hand slide from the small of her back to cup her bottom. She groaned in delight.

From the dimmest recesses of her mind Savannah realized that the room had grown ominously quiet. She reluctantly dragged her lips away from Knox's and saw the instructor grinning broadly at them.

"It looks like Knox and his wife have passed our little test with flying colors," the woman announced, her eyes twinkling knowingly. "No further instruction on this subject seems to be necessary."

Dear Reader,

While cruising the Internet looking at sex toys—research for my first Blaze novel, *Just Toying Around...* I swear!—the same word kept popping up. Tantra, or Tantric. Intrigued, I decided to do a little investigating and discovered that Tantric sex, though I'd never heard of it, had been around since 3000 B.C. and despite its dusty spiritual heritage, was swiftly gaining new popularity. It didn't take long to imagine a hero and heroine getting caught up in the mystical world of *Tantra,* and thus Knox and Savannah's story was born.

Journalist Knox Webber needs a weekend lover with one special requirement—he can't be attracted to her. Knox is on the scent of a great story, but in order to prove the touted Tantric way, which promises heightened awareness, spiritual gratification and hourlong full-body orgasms, is nothing but a farce, Knox needs to attend one of the popular Tantric Sex Clinics on the West Coast...and he needs a partner who won't distract him from his main goal—getting the story.

Savannah Reeves—his archenemy—fits the bill perfectly. But as the weekend progresses, sexual tension between them explodes and the resulting heat soon burns up all preconceived notions about the ancient art of lovemaking. Chemistry or Tantra, they wonder...and will it last once the weekend is over?

I hope you enjoy Knox and Savannah's sexy romantic romp.

Enjoy!

Rhonda Nelson

Books by Rhonda Nelson

HARLEQUIN BLAZE
75—JUST TOYING AROUND...

SHOW & TELL

Rhonda Nelson

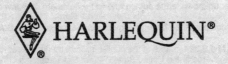

TORONTO • NEW YORK • LONDON
AMSTERDAM • PARIS • SYDNEY • HAMBURG
STOCKHOLM • ATHENS • TOKYO • MILAN • MADRID
PRAGUE • WARSAW • BUDAPEST • AUCKLAND

Once upon a time there was a towheaded, chubby-cheeked, demonic little prankster who grew into one of the best-looking, most hardworking, kindhearted and admirable men I have ever known—my brother, Greg Moore.

Being smarter than 98 percent of the population called for a great dedication, eh, Bubba?

ISBN 0-373-79085-6

SHOW & TELL

Copyright © 2003 by Rhonda Nelson.

Visit us at www.eHarlequin.com

1

KNOX WEBBER ABSENTLY SWIRLED the liquor around his glass as he watched the naked couple displayed on his television screen gyrate in sexual ecstasy. They sat in a pool of fuzzy golden light, face to face, palm to palm, the woman's hips anchored around the man's waist. Her long blond hair shimmered over her bare shoulders. She threw her head back and her mouth formed a perfect O of orgasmic wonder. The video's hypnotic narrator droned from the hi-fi speakers placed strategically around Knox's plush glass-and-chrome apartment.

"Let the tantric energy flow. You'll feel the power wash over you, through you and around you as your male and female energies merge. This wave of utter bliss will transport you and your partner to a new plane in sexual rapture, a new plane of enlightenment and awareness, where you'll flow in harmony with your lover and the rest of the world. Synchronized, controlled breathing is essential…"

Sheesh.

Knox snorted and hit the stop button on his remote control. He'd seen enough. He'd watched the how-to video on one of the best home-theater systems money could buy—a fifty-five-inch digitally mastered screen with superior resolution, picture in picture, and quality sound—and he still thought the entire concept of tantric sex was a load of crap.

Regrettably, it was becoming an increasingly popular load of crap and it just might be the one story he'd been looking for, the one pivotal article that would give him an edge over his competitors. Knox currently enjoyed a top spot in the Chicago scene of investigative journalism, but it wasn't enough. He wanted more. He wanted a Pulitzer. A wry smile twisted his lips. Granted, this story most likely wouldn't win him the coveted award, but it could put him that much closer to his goal. The thought sent a shot of adrenaline coursing through his blood.

Call it journalistic intuition, all he knew was each time Knox caught the scent of a good story, he'd get a curious feeling in his gut, an insistent nudge behind his naval that, so far, had never steered him wrong. This sixth sense had propelled him into his current comfortable position with the *Chicago Phoenix*, had earned him a reputation for staying on the cutting edge of journalism and keeping his finger on the fickle pulse of American society.

The nudge was there now, more insistent than ever, prodding him into action. But for the first time in his life, for reasons that escaped him, he found himself resisting the urge to pick up the scent and track down the story.

Knox chalked up his misgivings to inconvenience. Naturally, in the course of his work, he'd been mightily inconvenienced and had never minded the hassle. It was all part and parcel of his chosen career path, the one he'd taken despite howling protests from his more professionally minded parents. His mother and father considered Knox's career choice beneath him and were still clinging to the hope that he'd eventually come to his senses and use his Ivy League education for a more distinguished career.

They'd have a long wait.

Knox was determined to make his mark in the competitive world of investigative journalism, no matter the inconveniences. This wasn't just a career; it was his identity, who he was. He was a show-and-tell journalist—he unearthed facts, then he showed them to the American public, told them in his own outspoken way and encouraged them to draw their own conclusions.

He'd hidden in small dark places and he'd assumed countless disguises, some of which were completely emasculating, Knox thought, shuddering as he recalled the transvestite debacle. He'd made it a point to befriend a scope of unwitting informants, from assistants to top city officials to the occasional pimp and small-time thug, and all species in between, creating a network of eyes much like the Argus of Greek mythology.

The idea of being inconvenienced didn't disturb Knox—it was the form of inconvenience he was concerned about. Knox preferred to work solo, but for this particular story, that simply wasn't an option.

He'd have to have a partner, and a female partner at that. A wry smile turned his lips. After all, he couldn't very well attend a tantric sex workshop with a man.

Knox studied the glossy tantric sex pamphlet once more. This clinic—Total Tantra Edification—in particular was his target. While some workshops were probably on the up-and-up, something about this one didn't feel quite right. Hadn't from the beginning when this idea had first taken hold. The little brochure was chock-full of glowing testimonials from happy couples who had sworn that the workshop had saved their marriages, had brought their flat-lined sex lives from the brink of death via the energized, intimate therapy. Women, in particular, seemed to be thrilled with the results, citing multiple orgasms and even female ejaculation.

And why not? Knox wondered with a crooked grin. The whole technique seemed geared toward female gratification—a new twist in and of itself. According to his research, men avoided physical ejaculation completely, thereby prolonging their erections, and instead strove for full-body inner orgasms. The blast without the shower, so to speak, Knox thought.

Expensive tantric weekend workshops were becoming almost as common on the West Coast as surfers at the beach. While they hadn't gained as much popularity on the East Coast, interest in the subject was nonetheless increasing. A popular cable music program recently polled eighteen- to twenty-four-year-olds, and when asked what sexual subject they'd most like to learn about, tantric sex topped the list.

No doubt about it, it was a timely story. The nudge tingled behind his navel once more.

In this case, it was also a load of New Age baloney taught by aging hippies in unbleached hemp togas bent on feathering their retirement nests. Knox was sure of it. He glanced at the so-called instructors featured on the inside page. Drs. Edgar and Rupali Shea smiled back at him, the picture of glowing serenity and marital bliss.

Knox didn't buy it for a moment.

Honestly? What self-respecting man would purposely deprive himself of an orgasm during sex and claim inner enlightenment was better? Knox snorted, knocked back the dregs of his Scotch. Not a real man. Not a man's man, anyway. Sex with no orgasm? It was like a hot-fudge sundae minus the hot fudge. Hell, what would be the point?

Certainly, without ejaculation a man could keep an erection longer. But as long as one didn't detonate upon entry, what difference did it make? As long as you didn't leave your partner in the lurch—unforgivably lazy in his opinion—what was the problem with racing toward release? With grabbing the brass ring?

Absolutely nothing. While the concept of tantric

sex had originated in India around 3000 B.C. and might have been genuinely used with a noble goal in mind, in today's time the technique had simply become a new twist on an old game designed to milk desperate couples out of their hard-earned money. Greedy, marketing-savvy businessmen had taken the concept and bastardized it into a hedonistic, spiritual fix-all.

Knox firmly intended to prove it and he couldn't do it alone. He'd have to have a partner.

Several possible candidates came to mind, but he systematically ruled them out. He didn't have a single female acquaintance who wouldn't expect his undivided attention, and this would be a business trip, not a weekend tryst celebrated with fine food and recreational sex. Complete focus would be mandatory in order to preserve the integrity of the story.

Knox liked sex as much as the next guy—he was a man, after all. It was his nature. And while the entire workshop would be centered around the technique of tantric sex, Knox knew better than to think he'd be able to do his job with any objectivity and be testing the theories at the same time. He'd have to have complete focus. So he'd have to take along a female who could appreciate the job he'd come there to do, and he could not—*absolutely could not*—be attracted to her.

Three beats passed before he knew the perfect woman for the job, and when the name surfaced, he involuntarily winced with dread—Savannah Reeves, his archenemy at the *Phoenix*.

The idea of having to share his byline with the infuriating know-it-all—honestly, the woman could strip bark off a tree with that tongue of hers—was almost enough to make Knox abandon the whole scenario, but he knew he couldn't.

He had to do this story.

This story would change his life. He could feel it. Couldn't explain it, but intuitively knew it all the same.

And if that meant spending a weekend with a woman whose seemingly sole goal in life was to annoy him, then so be it. Knox could handle it. All modesty aside, he could handle just about any woman. A quick smile, a clever compliment and— voilà!—she was his.

But not Savannah. Never Savannah.

She seemed charm-proof. Knox frowned, studied the empty cut-glass tumbler he held loosely in his hand. The one and only time he'd attempted the old routine on Savannah, she'd given him a blast of sleet with those icy blue eyes of hers and laughed in his face. His cheeks burned with remembered humiliation. He'd never repeated the mistake. It had been a lesson well learned and, while he didn't outright avoid her—he wouldn't give her the satisfaction— he'd made a conscious effort to steer clear of her path. She…unnerved him.

Nevertheless, he seriously doubted that she'd let

her personal dislike of him keep her from jumping at the chance of a great story. Since she'd joined the staff a little over a year ago, she'd made it a point to usurp prime articles from him, to try to keep one step ahead of him. He'd never had any real competition at the *Phoenix* until her arrival. Though she irritated the hell out of him with her knowing little smiles and acid comments, the rivalry nonetheless kept him sharp, kept him on his toes.

Knox thoughtfully tapped the brochure against his thigh and once more reflected on his options...and realized he really only had one—Savannah. She was the only woman who fit the bill. Though he thoroughly dreaded it, he'd have to ask her to accompany him on the trip to California, to play the part of his devoted sex partner. A bark of dry laughter erupted from his throat. Oh, she'd love that, he thought with a grim smile.

Generally speaking, Knox was attracted to just about every woman of the right age with a halfway decent rack. Shallow, yes, but, again, his nature. He couldn't help himself. He didn't always act on the attraction—in fact, he was quite selective with his lovers—but it was always there, hovering just beneath the surface.

Regardless of his hyperlibido, Knox didn't doubt for one minute that one icy look, one chilly smile from the admittedly gorgeous Savannah Reeves would wilt even his staunchest erection. Savannah was petite and curvy with short jet-black hair that always looked delightfully rumpled. Like she'd just rolled out of bed. She wore little makeup, but with a smooth, creamy complexion and that pair of ice-blue eyes heavily fringed with long curling lashes, she hardly needed the artifice. No doubt about it, she was definitely gorgeous, Knox admitted as he forced away her distracting image.

But looks weren't everything.

Regrettably, Savannah Reeves had the personality of a constipated toad and never missed her daily ration of Bitch Flakes. Knox suppressed a shudder.

He definitely wouldn't have to worry about being attracted to her. He simply wouldn't allow it. And she certainly wasn't attracted to him—she'd gone out of her way to make that abundantly clear. Also she'd likely appreciate being in on the job.

In short, she'd be his perfect partner for this assignment. And she was too glory hungry to let a little thing like personal dislike get in the way of a fantastic byline. If he really wanted to, Knox thought consideringly, he could make her wriggle like a worm on a hook.

The idea held immense appeal.

"NOT NO, BUT HELL NO," Savannah Reeves said flatly as she wound her way through the busy newsroom to her little cubicle.

Knox, damn him, dogged her every step.

"But why not? It's a plum assignment, a great

story and a wonderful opportunity. What possible reason could you have for saying no?''

Because I don't like you, Savannah thought uncharitably. She drew up short beside her desk and paused to look at him. She fought the immediate impulse to categorize his finer physical features, but, as usual, failed miserably.

Knox Webber had wavy rich brown hair cut in a negligent style that implied little maintenance but undoubtedly took several time-consuming steps to achieve. His eyes were a dark, verdant green, heavy-lidded, and twinkled with mischief and the promise of wicked pleasures. His lips, which seemed perpetually curled into an inviting come-hither grin, were surprisingly full for a man, but masculine enough to make a woman fantasize about their talent.

Even her, dammit, though she should know better.

If that weren't enough, he had the absolute best ass she'd ever seen—tight and curved just so and… Savannah resisted the urge to shiver. In addition to that amazing ass, he was tall, athletically built and carried himself with a mesmerizing long-limbed, loose-hipped gait that drew the eye and screamed confidence. He'd been born into a family of wealth and privilege and the very essence of that breeding hovered like an aura about him.

Though she knew it was unreasonable, Savannah immediately felt her defenses go up. She'd been orphaned at six when her parents had been killed in a car accident. With no other family, she'd spent her childhood in the foster-care system, passed from family to family like a yard-sale castoff. Did Knox know how lucky he'd been? Did he have any idea at all? She didn't think so. From what she'd observed, he seemed content to play the black sheep of the family—to *play* at being a journalist—until his father turned the screws and capped his sizable trust fund. And the hell of it was, Knox made it all look so damned easy. He was a talented bastard, she'd give him that. It was enough to make her retch.

"Come on, Vannah," Knox cajoled, using the nickname that never failed to set her teeth on edge. He was the only person at the *Phoenix* who dared call her that and the implied intimacy of the nickname drove her mad. "This is going to be a helluva story."

She didn't doubt that for one minute. Knox Webber didn't waste his time on anything that didn't promise a front page. And he had to be desperate to ask her for help, because she knew he'd rather slide buck naked down a razor blade into a pool of alcohol than ask her for a favor.

Still, there was no way in hell she wanted any part of a story with him, phenomenal byline or no. She didn't have to possess any psychic ability to know that the outcome could be nothing short of disastrous. An extended weekend at a sex workshop with Knox? The one and only man she didn't have a prayer of resisting? The one she continually fantasized about? A vision of her and Knox naked and sweaty loomed instantly in her mind's eye, making her tummy quiver with perpetually repressed longing.

No way.

Savannah firmed her chin and repeated her last thought for his benefit. "Forget it, Knox. Ask someone else." She gave him her back once more and slid into the chair behind her desk.

"I don't want to ask anyone else. I've asked you." Knox frowned at her and the expression was so uncharacteristic that it momentarily startled her. Savannah blinked, then gathered her wits about her.

"I can't believe you won't even consider it," the object of her irritation repeated stubbornly. "I thought you'd jump at the chance to have a go at this story."

Savannah tsked. "I warned you about that. Thinking upsets the delicate balance of your constitution. Best to avoid the process at all costs, Webber."

He muttered something that sounded suspiciously like "smart-ass," but Savannah couldn't be sure.

Still he was right. Had any other male co-worker asked her, she wouldn't have hesitated. In fact, it was almost frightening how much their minds thought alike. She'd been toying with the idea of a tantric sex article for a couple of weeks now and had been waiting for the concept to gel. She'd simply let him get the jump on her this time—a rare feat, because she'd made a game out of thwarting him.

"You don't know what it is, do you?" Wearing an infuriating little grin Savannah itched to slap off his face, Knox leaned his incredible ass against her desk.

"Know what *what* is?" Her eyes rounded. *"Sex?"* With an indelicate snort, Savannah booted up her laptop and did her best to appear unaware of him. "Granted, I might not have as much experience as you—I'm sure you'd give the hookers in the red-light district a run for their money in the experience department—but I'm not completely ignorant, for pity's sake," Savannah huffed. She cast him an annoyed glance. "I know what sex is."

Though it had been so long since she'd had any, her memory was getting a little fuzzy about the particulars. If she didn't get laid soon, she'd undoubtedly be declared a virgin again simply by default. Or out of pity. Twelve- to fourteen-hour workdays didn't leave much time for romance. Besides, after Gibson Lyles III, Savannah didn't put much stock in romance, or in men, for that matter. She sighed. Men were too much work, for too little reward.

"Not just sex," Knox said. *"Tantric sex.* Do you know what it is?"

Savannah loaded her web browser, busying herself with the task at hand. "Sure. It's a complex marriage of yoga, ritual, meditation and intercourse."

Alternately, he looked surprised then impressed. "Very good. See? You're perfect."

"Be that as it may, I'm not going. I have work to do. Go away." Savannah smoothed her hair behind her ears and continued to pretend he wasn't there.

No small feat when every single part of her tingled as a result of his nearness. Which sucked, particularly since, for the most part, she couldn't stand him. *"Go away,"* she repeated.

Knox continued to study her and another maddening twinkle lit his gaze. "I see. You're scared."

Savannah resisted the urge to grind her teeth. "Scared of what?"

"Of me, obviously." Knox picked an imaginary fleck of lint from the cuff of his expensive shirt. "Why else would you refuse such a great opportunity when it's painfully obvious that you've been considering the topic as well?" Something shifted in his gaze. "That…or you're into it."

"Ooh, you've found me out. Good job, Columbo. And don't flatter yourself. I am *not* afraid of you." Savannah chuckled. "I've got your number, Slick. Nothing about you frightens me." Savannah figured providence would promptly issue a bolt of lightning and turn her into a Roman candle for that whopper, but thankfully she remained spark free.

The silence lengthened until Knox finally blew out an impatient breath. "Won't you even consider it?"

"No."

His typically amiable expression vanished. "This is a great opportunity. Don't make me play hardball."

Exasperated, Savannah leveled a hard look at him. "Play whatever kind of ball you want, Knox. But you won't make me play with you. I'm not one of your newsroom groupies. Now get out of my cubby—you're crowding me.''

Wearing a look of supreme frustration, Knox finally stalked off, presumably to ask another female to do his bidding. Good riddance, Savannah thought, though she did hate the missed opportunity.

But even had she been inclined to accept the offer, she really wouldn't have had the time to pursue the assignment—groveling to Chapman, her diabolical boss, and covering all of the demeaning little stories he gleefully threw her way were taking up entirely too much of her time.

Savannah and Chapman were presently embroiled in the proverbial Mexican standoff, neither of them willing to budge. The problem revolved around a libel suit that had been filed against the *Chicago Phoenix* as a result of one of her stories. To Chapman's extreme irritation and despite various threats, Savannah stood by her story and refused to compromise her journalistic integrity by revealing her source. Chapman had bullied and blustered, wailed and threatened everything from being demoted to being fired, but Savannah simply would not relent. Her credibility would be ruined. To give up this source would ultimately wreck her career.

Besides, it was just wrong. She'd given her word and she wouldn't compromise her integrity simply for the sake of the paper. That's why they employed high-powered attorneys. Let them sort it out. She'd only been doing her job, and she'd done it to the absolute best of her ability. She refused to admit any wrongdoing, and she'd be damned before she'd claim any responsibility.

Savannah had been educated in the school of hard knocks, had been on her own since she'd turned eighteen and was no longer a ward of the state. She'd put herself through college by working three grueling jobs. Sure, covering the opening of a new strip mall was degrading, but if Hugh Chapman thought he could get the better of her by giving her crappy assignments, then he had another think coming. She stiffened her spine. Savannah was certain she was tough enough to take anything her mean-spirited boss could dish out.

Don't make me play hardball.

A premonition of dread surfaced as Knox's parting comment tripped unexpectedly through her mind.

She was wrong, Savannah decided. She was tough enough to take anything *but* a weekend sex workshop with Knox Webber.

2

"...SO YOU SEE, this story has incredible potential. I have it on good authority that the *Tribune* is considering the angle as well."

Predictably, Hugh Chapman, editor in chief of the *Chicago Phoenix* bristled when taunted with the prospect of their rival paper possibly getting a scoop.

"You don't say," the older man grunted thoughtfully. As tall as he was wide, with large fishlike eyes, thick lips, a bulbous nose and pasty complexion, Chapman bore an unfortunate resemblance to an obese albino guppy. But Hugh Chapman was no harmless fish. He'd been in the publishing business for years and Knox didn't think he'd ever met a man more shrewd or calculating. Vindictive even, if the rumors were true.

Playing him was risky, but Knox desperately needed to do this story and he'd already tried the ethical route. It hadn't worked, so he'd been forced to employ a different tactic. His conscience twinged, but Knox ignored it. He'd given Savannah a chance to make the trip to California of her own accord.

She'd refused. If Knox played his cards right, in just a few minutes she'd wish she hadn't.

Knox heaved a dramatic sigh. "Yeah, I'm afraid so. I'd really like to get the jump on them. Pity Savannah didn't go for the idea," Knox said regretfully. "And I can't do it without her. Oh, well. You win some, you lose some. I'm sure we'll beat them to the punch on something else." Knox smacked his hands on his thighs, seemingly resigned, and started to stand.

"Call her in here," Chapman said abruptly.

With an innocent look, Knox paused. "Sorry?"

"I said call her in here. You need her to go—I'll make her go." His beefy brow folded in consternation. "Presently, Ms. Reeves is in no position to refuse me. She's skating on thin ice as it is."

"Oh, sir, I don't know," Knox protested. "I didn't—"

"Webber, do what I told you to do," Chapman barked.

"Right, sir." Knox's step was considerably lighter as he crossed the room and pulled the glass door open. "Savannah Reeves, Mr. Chapman would like to see you."

Savannah's head appeared from behind her cubby. Knox's triumphant expression combined with the boss's summons seemed to register portents of doom because, within seconds, her pale blue eyes narrowed to angry slits and her lips flattened into a tense line.

She stood and made her way across the room. Tension vibrated off her slight form.

"I told you not to make me play hardball," Knox murmured silkily as she drew near.

"If you've done what I think you've done," she returned with a brittle smile, obviously for the benefit of onlookers, since she clearly longed to strangle him, "you will be *so* very sorry. I will permanently extinguish your 'wand of light.'"

Knox choked on a laugh as she swept past into the inner sanctum of Chapman's office. In traditional tantra, the Sanskrit word for penis was *lingam,* which translated into "wand of light." She certainly knew her stuff, Knox thought, surprised and impressed once more with her knowledge of the subject. He'd been right in forcing her hand. Annoying though she may be—the bane of his professional existence—Savannah Reeves was a crackerjack journalist. Very thorough.

"You wanted to see me, sir," Savannah said.

Knox moved to stand beside Savannah, who seemed determined to pretend he didn't exist. She kept her gaze focused on Chapman and refused to acknowledge Knox at all. His conscience issued another screech for having her called on the carpet, but he determinedly ignored the howl. If she had simply used her head and agreed, this could have all been avoided. It was her own fault.

Chapman gave her a long, unyielding stare, so hard that Knox himself was hard-pressed not to flinch. His scalp suddenly prickled with unease. What was it Chapman had said? She was on thin ice? Why? Knox wondered instantly. Why was she on thin ice?

"I understand Knox has asked you to accompany him on an extended weekend assignment and you have refused," Chapman said.

She nodded. "Yes, sir. That's correct."

Chapman steepled his fingers so that they looked like little pork sausages. "I'm not going to ask you why you refused, because that would imply that I care and I don't—that you have a choice, and you don't. You will go. Understood?"

She stiffened. "But, sir—"

Chapman's forehead formed a unibrowed scowl. "No buts." He looked meaningfully at Knox. "Surely it's not going to be necessary for me to remind you of why it would behoove you not to argue with me about this."

Though she clearly longed to do just that, Savannah's shoulders rounded with uncharacteristic defeat. She sighed. "No, sir. Of course not."

Knox frowned. What in hell was going on? How had she managed to land her name on the top of Chapman's shit-list? What had she done? he wondered again.

"That's what I thought. Knox," Chapman said, "see Rowena and have her tend to the necessary arrangements." He nodded at Savannah. "The two of you should get together and make your plans."

Knox smiled. "Right, sir. Thank you."

Savannah didn't say a word, just turned and marched rigidly out of the office. Knox had to double-time it to catch up with her. "What was that all ab—"

"That," Savannah said meaningfully, "is none of your business, but that's probably never stopped you before. Honestly, I can't believe that you did that— that you went to Chapman." She shook her head. "I knew you were a spoiled little tight-ass and a first-rate jerk, but it honestly never occurred to me that you'd sink so damned low."

Knox scowled at the tight-ass remark but refused to let her goad him, and followed her into her cubicle once more. "In case you haven't noticed," Knox pointed out sarcastically, "it's our job to make *everything* our business. That's what journalists do. Besides, I gave you the opportunity to do the right thing."

She blasted him with a frosty glare. "Wrong. You gave me the opportunity to do what *you* wanted me to do." Savannah shoved a hand through her hair impatiently, mussing it up even more. She took a deep breath, clearly trying to calm herself but failing miserably. She opened her mouth. Shut it. Opened it again. Finally she said, "Did it ever occur to you that I might have plans for this weekend? That it might not be convenient for me to jaunt off to California with you?"

Prepared to argue with whatever insult she hurled

next, that question caught him completely off guard and Knox felt his expression blank.

"I thought so." She collapsed into her chair. "You pampered prep-school boys are all the same. Contrary to popular belief, Mr. Webber, the world does not revolve around you and your every whim." She laughed, but the sound lacked humor. "We peasants have lives to."

Peasants? Knox scrubbed a hand over his face and felt a flush creep up his neck. She was right. He hadn't considered that she'd have any plans. He'd just assumed that, like him, work didn't leave time for anything else. "Look, I'm sorry for wrecking your plans. That was never my intention. I just—"

"You didn't wreck my plans, because I didn't have any," she said tartly. She turned back to her computer, doing her best to ignore him out of existence.

Knox blinked. Felt his fingers curl into his palms. "If you didn't have any plans, then what the hell is the problem?" he asked tightly.

"I *could* have had plans. It's just a lucky coincidence that I don't."

Knox blew out a breath. "Whatever. When would you like to get together and see to the details of this trip?"

She snorted. "Never."

"Vannah…" Knox warned, feeling his patience wear thin.

"*Savannah,*" she corrected, and he could have

sworn he heard one of her teeth crack. "You can brief me on the plane. Until then, get away from me and leave me alone."

"But—"

She glanced up from her computer. "You might have won the battle, but you certainly haven't won the war. You've forced my hand, but that's all I'm going to allow. Do not speak to me again until we're on our way to California or, Chapman's edict or no, you'll be making the journey solo."

A hot oath sizzled on Knox's tongue, but he bit back the urge. He'd never met a woman who infuriated him more, and the desire to call her bluff was almost overpowering.

But he didn't.

He couldn't afford the risk. This story meant too much. He knew it and he needed to keep the bigger picture in focus.

Instead, though it galled him to no end, Knox nodded succinctly and wordlessly left her cubicle.

SAVANNAH HAD SILENTLY PRAYED that Knox would screw up and talk to her so that she could make good on her threat, but he didn't. Per her instruction, he hadn't said a single word to her until they boarded the plane. Since then he'd seemed determined to treat this assignment like any other, and even more determined to ignore the fact that she'd been an unwilling participant.

A typical man, Savannah thought. If he couldn't

buy it off, knock it down or bully it aside, then he ignored it.

They'd flown out of O'Hare at the ungodly hour of five in the morning and would arrive in sunny Sacramento, California, by nine-thirty. At the airport, they would rent a car to finish the journey. The Shea compound was located in the small community of Riverdale, about fifty miles northwest of Sacramento. Barring any unforeseen complications, they should arrive in plenty of time to get settled and attend the Welcome Brunch. Classes officially started at two.

A volcano of dread erupted in her belly at the thought, but rather than allow it to consume her, Savannah channeled her misgivings into a more productive emotion—anger.

She still saw red every time she thought about Chapman's hand in her humiliation. Quite honestly, she'd been surprised that he hadn't taken every opportunity to belittle her in front of her co-workers—to make an example of her—and could only assume he acted on the advice of the paper's attorneys. Chapman seemed the type to feed off others' misfortune, and, frankly, she'd never liked him. She wasn't the least bit surprised that Chapman had sided with Knox. Knox was the golden boy, after all.

But the *Phoenix* had an unparalleled reputation, and she would have been insane not to accept employment at one of the most prestigious papers in the States. She had her career plan, after all, and wouldn't let a little thing like despising her boss get in the way. Though she assumed he'd never give her a glowing recommendation, her writing would speak for itself.

As for Knox's role in this…she was still extremely perturbed at him for not taking no for an answer. Without a family or mentor to speak of, Savannah relied solely on gut instinct. She had to. She didn't have a choice. In the absence of one perception, others became heightened, supersensitized. Just as the blind had a keener sense of smell, she'd developed a keener sense of perception, of self-preservation. When Knox had walked up and asked her to share this story with him, her knee-jerk gut reaction had been swift and telling—she'd almost tossed her cookies.

Going on this trip with him was the height of stupidity. Savannah could be brutally honest with herself when the need arose and she knew beyond a shadow of a doubt that this attraction to Knox was a battle she could not win. If Knox so much as touched her, she'd melt, and then he'd know her mortifying secret—that she'd been lusting after him for over a year.

Savannah bit back a wail of frustration, resisted the childish urge to beat her head against the small oval window. She didn't need to be here with him—she needed to be back in Chicago. Investigating the missing maintenance hole cover Chapman would have undoubtedly assigned her next. Watering her plants. Straightening her stereo wires, her canned goods.

Anything but being here with Knox.

Though she'd been making a concerted effort to imagine him away from the seat next to hers, Savannah was still hammeringly aware of him. She could feel the heat from his body, could smell the mixture of fine cologne and his particular essence. The fine hairs on her arms continually prickled, seemed magnetically drawn to him. Savannah surreptitiously studied him, traced the angular curve of his jaw with her gaze, the smooth curve of his lips. A familiar riptide of longing washed through her and sensual fantasies rolled languidly through the private cinema of her mind. She suppressed a sigh. No doubt about it, he was a handsome devil.

And due to some hideous character flaw on her own part—or just plain ignorance, she couldn't be sure—she was in lust with him. The panting, salivating, wanna-rip-your-clothes-off-and-do-it-in-the-elevator, trisexual—meaning "try *anything*"—type. Had been from the very first moment she'd laid eyes on him the day she joined the staff at the *Phoenix*.

Of course, he'd screwed it all up by opening his mouth.

Thanks to Gibson Lyles III, Savannah recognized the cool, modulated tones of those born to wealth. There'd been other signs as well, but initially she'd been so bowled over by her physical reaction to him that she hadn't properly taken them into consideration. The wardrobe, the posture, the polish. It had all been there once she'd really looked. And one look had been all it had taken for her to delegate him to her *hell-no* list. Since then she'd looked for flaws, probably exaggerated a few, and had not permitted herself to so much as like him.

Savannah knew what happened when rich boys took poor orphans home to meet the parents. Her lips twisted into a derisive smile. The rich boy got an all-expenses-paid tour of Europe…and the poor orphan got backhanded by reality.

Thanks, but no thanks.

Frustration peaked once more. Why had he demanded that she come? Why her, dammit? There were other female journalists employed at the *Phoenix,* other women just as qualified. What had been so special about her that none of the others would do?

When Savannah contemplated what this extended weekend would entail, all the talk of sex, having to share a room with him, for pity's sake, it all but overwhelmed her. How on earth would she keep her appalling attraction for him secret during a hands-on sex workshop? What, pray tell, would prevent her from becoming a single, pulsing, throbbing nerve of need? How would she resist him?

She wouldn't, she knew. If he so much as crooked a little finger in invitation, she'd be hopelessly, utterly and completely lost.

Savannah knew a few basic truths about the art of tantric sex, knew the male and female roles. Knew that the art of intimate massage, of prolonged fore-play and ritual were particularly stressed themes throughout the process. But that was only the tip of the iceberg. There were other, more intimidating—and intimate—themes prevalent as well.

Tantrists believed that humans possessed six chak-ras—or sources of energy—and that during life, these energy sources got blocked due to the traumas humans suffered. But once these chakras were unblocked, and energy was free to move as it should, then when the male and female bodies merged, these energies merged as well, creating a oneness with a partner that transcended the physical and, thus, turned sex into a spiritual experience.

But how could a person take it seriously? Take some of the lingo for instance. His penis was a "wand of light." The Sanskrit word for vagina was *yoni,* which translated to "sacred space."

Please.

Who could say this stuff to their partner with a straight face? Sorry. She just couldn't see herself looking deeply into the eyes of her lover and saying, *Welcome to my sacred space. Illuminate me, baby, with your wand of light!*

Frankly Savannah didn't know what tact Knox wanted to take with this story, but she thought the whole idea was ludicrous. She liked her sex hot, frantic and sweaty and she didn't want to learn an ancient language to do the business either. Honestly, whatever happened to the good old-fashioned quickie?

She supposed she should give the premise the benefit of the doubt—that was her job, after all—but she seriously doubted that a massage and a few chants thrown in amid the usual twenty-minute flesh session would result in a spiritual experience for her. She liked the rub, lick and tickle approach, thank you very much. But to each his own, she supposed.

Knox elbowed her. "Hey, would you like anything to drink?"

Savannah started, then turned to see that the stewardess had arrived with the refreshment cart. "Uh…sure. A soda would be nice."

"Ditto," Knox said. He upped the charm voltage with a sexy little smile. "And an extra pack of peanuts, too, if you've got any to spare."

The flight attendant blushed and obligingly handed over the requested snack. Savannah rolled her eyes. And women were accused of using feminine wiles? What about men? What about masculine wiles? Knox, for example, had just dazzled that woman with nothing more than a little eye contact and a well-turned smile.

"Want some peanuts?" Knox asked, offering the open pack to her.

"No, thank you."

Knox paused to look at her and sighed. "What have I done now?"

Savannah inserted the straw into her drink. "I don't know what you're talking about."

"Sure you do. The temperature around your seat

has dropped to an arctic level, when, just moments ago, I was enjoying the chilly-but-above-freezing climes of your sunny disposition." He smiled, the wretch. "Clearly, I've offended you once again. Don't be shy. Go ahead. Tell me what odious man-thing I'm guilty of now."

Savannah felt her lips twitch but managed to suppress a grin. "You're breathing."

Knox chuckled, a low rumbling sound that made his arm brush against hers and sent a shower of sensation fizzing up her arm. Savannah closed her eyes and pulled in a slow breath.

"I'm afraid I'm not going to attempt to remedy that offense," he told her. "I like breathing. Breathing is best for my continued good health."

"So is leaving me alone."

"Come on, Savannah. How long are you going to keep this up?"

"Dunno." She pulled a thoughtful face. "Depends on how long I'm going to have to work with you."

"Can't you even admit that this is going to be one helluva story? A coup for both of us?"

He was right. She'd grown increasingly weary of covering the mundane, was ready for a real assignment. Still...

"I don't have a problem with admitting that at all. I just don't like your methods. It was high-handed and sneaky, and I don't appreciate being made a pawn in the game of your career."

Knox shifted in his seat, then emptied the rest of

the peanuts down his throat and finished the last of his drink before he responded. "Sorry," he mumbled.

Savannah blinked and turned to face him. "Come again?"

"I said I was sorry," Knox repeated in a little bit stronger voice.

Savannah widened her eyes in mock astonishment, cupped her hand around her ear and made an exaggerated show of not hearing him correctly. "Sorry, didn't catch that? What did you say again?"

"I said I was sorry!" Knox hissed impatiently. He plowed a hand through his carefully gelled hair, clearly out of his comfort zone when issuing an apology. "I shouldn't have gone to Chapman. But you didn't leave me any choice. I have to do *this* story and I needed *you* to go with me."

"Why me?" Savannah demanded quietly, finally getting to the heart of the matter. "Why not Claire or Whitney? Why did it have to be me?"

"Because I…" Knox swallowed, strangely reluctant to finish the thought.

"Because you what?" Savannah persisted.

He finally blew out a breath. "Because I couldn't take anyone with me who might be attracted to me. Or that I might be attracted to."

Slack-jawed, for a moment Savannah was too stunned to be insulted. She managed a smirk, even as dismay mushroomed inside her belly. "That irresistible, are you?"

"No, not to you," he huffed impatiently. His cheeks reddened. "You don't have any trouble at all resisting me. Hell, you've made a point of ensuring that I know just how resistible to you I am. *You* were the only logical choice. We have to stay focused, to remain objective. If I had asked any other woman at the *Phoenix* to make this trip with me, then you know as well as I do that they would have considered it a come-on. An invitation for seduction." He smiled without humor. "Did that occur to *you?*"

Savannah had readied her mouth for a cool put-down, but found herself curiously unable to come up with one. He was right. The idea of him wanting to seduce her had never crossed her mind—she'd been too worried about how hard it would be not to seduce him.

She'd known that he'd never been romantically interested in her—she'd purposely cultivated a hate-hate relationship with him to avoid that very scenario. Savannah knew she should be pleased with how well her plan had worked, but she found herself perversely unable to work up any enthusiasm for her success. He'd chosen her because she'd led him to believe that she wasn't attracted to him and because he, by his own admission, wasn't attracted to her.

All of that effort for this...this nightmare.

Irony could be a class-A bitch, Savannah thought wearily.

"Are we going to be able to get past this and work together?" he asked.

Savannah heaved a put-upon sigh. "Yeah…so long as you don't pull a show-and-tell session with your 'wand of light.'" She inwardly harrumphed. Didn't look like that would be a problem. And she was happy about it, dammit. This was a good thing. Really. She didn't want him to be attracted to her, any more than she wanted to be attracted to him.

Knox grinned, one of those baby-the-things-I-could-do-to-you smiles that made a woman's brain completely lose reason—including hers. "Let's make a deal. I won't show you mine unless you show me yours."

Savannah smirked, even as she suppressed a shiver. "Well, that'll be simple enough—*I* don't have a 'wand of light.'" She nodded succinctly. "Deal."

A sexy chuckle rumbled from his chest. "Deal."

3

"ARE YOU READY to discuss our cover?" Knox asked, when he'd finally navigated the rental car out onto the busy freeway.

He would have liked to cover everything while in the air where she couldn't have done him any bodily injury, but after his bungled apology, she'd feigned sleep for the rest of the flight. Knox didn't feel quite as safe in the car and he grimly suspected she wasn't going to care for the cover story he'd devised for the two of them. He'd made the mistake of filling out the application and accompanying questionnaire while still angry with her. Knox winced as he recalled the uncharitable things he'd had to say about his "wife's" shortcomings in bed.

She'd undoubtedly kill him.

Savannah fished her sunglasses from her purse and slid them into place. She'd dressed for travel in a sleeveless sky-blue linen pantsuit that perfectly matched the startling shade of her eyes and showed her small, curvy form to advantage. She wore simple diamond studs in her ears and her short black locks were delightfully mussed. Her lipstick had worn off hours ago, but refreshingly unlike most females, she didn't seem to mind.

Knox was still trying to decide how much to tell her about their cover story when she said, "Sure, go ahead and fill me in."

He swallowed and strove for a nonchalant tone. "We're registered as Mr. and Mrs. Knox Weston. Your first name is Barbie. We've been having a little—"

"*Barbie?*"

Knox winced at her shrill exclamation. "That's right."

With a withering smirk, she crossed her arms over her chest and turned to face him. "And why is my first name Barbie?"

Knox cast about his paralyzed mind for some sort of plausible lie, but couldn't come up with anything halfway believable and settled for the truth. "Because I was pissed and knew you would hate it." He threw her a sidelong glance and was pleased that he'd been able to—it meant that he still had his eyes and she hadn't scratched them out yet. "It was a petty thrill. I regret it now, of course," he quickly imparted at her venomous look. "But what's done is done and I can't very well tell them that I've made a mistake, that I didn't know my own wife's name." He forced a chuckle. "That would look pretty odd."

Looking thoroughly put out, Savannah studied him until Knox was hard-pressed not to squirm. "A petty thrill, eh?" She humphed. "Is there anything else—

besides my name—that you might have falsely reported about me? Anything else I should know about?''

He shifted uncomfortably. ''Er—''

''Knox…'' Savannah said threateningly.

Knox considered taking the next exit. If she went ballistic and attacked him, he didn't want any innocent bystanders to be hurt. ''Well, just for the sake of our cover, you understand, they, uh…might think that you're frigid and unable to reach climax.''

Knox heard her outraged gasp and tensed, readied himself for a blow.

''Well, that can be easily explained,'' she said frostily, ''when I tell them that you're a semi-impotent premature ejaculator.''

Knox quailed and resisted the natural urge to adjust himself, to assure himself that everything was in working order. ''Well, I—I can hardly see where that will b-be necessary,'' he croaked. ''One of us had to have a problem or we wouldn't have needed the workshop in the first place.'' A good, rational argument, Knox thought, congratulating himself.

She laughed. ''Oh, I see. And *I* just had to be the one with the problem? Why couldn't *you* have been the one with the problem?''

''Because I—''

She chuckled. ''Because you're such a stud that the idea of your equipment not passing muster—even fictitiously—was too much for your poor primitive male mind to comprehend. How pathetically juvenile." She smiled. "Do continue. We'll be there soon and I want to make sure that I'm completely in character."

Knox frowned at the words "pathetically juvenile," but under the circumstances, he let it pass. He cleared his throat and did his best to maintain his train of thought. "We've been married for two years and have never been completely satisfied with our, er, sex life. We're looking for something more and long for a closer relationship with one another. Our marriage is on the rocks as a result of our failure to communicate in the bedroom."

She snorted. "Because I'm frigid."

"Er…right."

"And you're impotent."

"Ri— Wrong!" Sheesh. A bead of sweat broke out on his upper lip. "That's, uh, not what our profile says."

"Because you filled it out. Look, Knox, if you think for one minute that I'm taking the total blame for our sorry sex life and our failing marriage during this farce, you'd better think again. You wanted this story, so you'd better damn well be ready to play your part. If I'm frigid, then, by God, you're going to be impotent."

Knox felt his balls shrivel up with dread. He set his jaw so hard he feared it would crack. She had to be the most competitive, argumentative female he'd ever encountered. The bigger picture, he reminded himself. Think of the bigger picture. "If you insist," he said tightly.

"I do."

"Fine." He blew out a breath. "There are still a few more things we need to go over. As for our occupations, I'm a veterinarian and you're my assistant."

She quirked a brow. "That's a bit of a stretch."

Smiling, Knox shrugged. "I got carried away."

Savannah's lips curled into a genuine smile, not the cynical smirk she usually wore, and the difference between the two was simply breathtaking. It was a sweet grin, devoid of any sentiment but real humor. To Knox's disquiet, he felt a buzz of heat hum along his spine.

"Be that as it may, I hope we're not called upon to handle a pet emergency," she said wryly. "I don't know the first thing about animals."

"What? No Spot or Fluffy in your past?"

A shadow passed over her face. "No, I'm afraid not."

Knox waited a beat to see if she would elaborate, and when she didn't, he filed that information away for future consideration and moved to fill the sudden silence. "Look in the front pocket of my laptop case, would you?"

Savannah turned and hefted the case from the back floorboard. She unzipped the front pouch. "What am I looking for? Your Viagra?"

"No." He smiled. "Just something to authenticate our marriage. Our rings are in there."

A line emerged between her brows and she paused to look at him. "Rings?"

Knox reached over, pilfered through the pocket and withdrew a couple of small velvet boxes. "Yeah, rings. Married people wear them. Fourth finger, left hand, closest to the heart."

"Ooh, I'm impressed. How does an impotent bachelor like you know all that sentimental swill?"

"I'm not impotent," Knox growled. "And I know because, having been best man at three different weddings in the past year, it's my business to know."

Savannah nodded. "Hmm."

"Hmm, what?" Knox asked suspiciously, casting her a sidelong glance.

She lifted one shoulder in a negligent shrug. "I'm surprised, that's all."

"Surprised that I've been a best man?"

"No, surprised that you had three male friends. I've never seen you with anyone but the opposite sex."

Knox shivered dramatically. "Oh, that's cold."

"Well, what do you expect? Us frigid unable-to-climax types are like that."

Smothering a smile, he tossed the smallest box to her. "Just put on your ring, Barbie."

Savannah lifted the lid and calmly withdrew the plain gold band. Anxiety knotted his gut. Though it had been completely unreasonable, Knox had found himself poring over tray after tray, trying to find the perfect band for her finger. He'd finally gotten disgusted with himself—they weren't really getting married, for Pete's sake—and had selected the simple unadorned band. Savannah didn't seem the type for flash and sparkle.

She seemed curiously reluctant to put it on, but finally slipped the ring over her knuckle and fitted it into place. She turned her hand this way and that. "It's lovely. And it fits perfectly. Good job, Knox. It had never occurred to me that we'd need rings. Where did you get these?"

With an inaudible sigh, Knox opened his own box, snagged his equally simple band and easily pushed it into place. "My jeweler, of course."

She winced. "Would have been cheaper to have gone to the pawnshop."

"Call me superstitious, but I didn't want to jinx this marriage—even a fake one—with unlucky bands."

"Unlucky bands?" she repeated dubiously.

"Yes. Unlucky. Think about it—if they'd been lucky they'd still be on their owners' fingers, not in a cheap fake-velvet tray in a pawnshop." He tsked. "Bad karma."

She chuckled, gazing at him with a curious expression not easily read. "You're right. You are superstitious."

"We're here," Knox announced needlessly. He

whistled low as he wheeled the rented sedan into a parking space in front of the impressive compound— *compound* meaning *mansion*. The nudge behind his navel gave another powerful jab as Knox gazed at the cool, elegant facade of the Shea's so-called compound. When Knox thought of a compound, rows of cheap low-slung utilitarian buildings came to mind. This was easily a million-dollar spread and there was nothing low-slung or utilitarian about the impressive residence before him.

The house, a bright, almost blindingly white stucco, was a two-story Spanish dream, with a red tiled roof and a cool, inviting porch that ran the length of the house. The front doors were a work of art in and of themselves, arched double mahogany wonders with an inlaid sunburst design in heavy leaded glass. Huge urns filled with bright flowering plants were scattered about the porch, along with several plush chaise longues and comfortable chairs.

Knox would have expected a place like this to have been professionally landscaped, but there was a whimsical, unplanned feel to the various shrubs and flora, as though the gardener had simply planted at will with no particular interest in traditional landscaping. There were no borders, no pavers, and no mulch to speak of, just clumps of flowers, greenery and the occasional odd shrub and ornamental tree. Julio, his parents' gardener, who was prone to a symmetrical design, would undoubtedly have an apoplectic fit if he saw this charmingly chaotic approach to landscaping.

"Quite a layout, huh?" Savannah murmured.

Knox nodded grimly. "Quite."

Savannah unbuckled her seat belt. "Before we go in, just what exactly is your opinion of tantric sex?"

Knox surveyed his surroundings once more. "In this case, I think it's a lucrative load of crap."

"For once we're in agreement."

A miracle, Knox thought, wondering how long the phenomenon would last. "Get your purse, Barbie. It's show time."

SAVANNAH ABSENTLY FIDGETED with the ring on her finger. It wasn't uncomfortable, just unfamiliar, and it fit perfectly. She covertly peeked at it again and a peculiar ache swelled in her chest. The smooth, cool band was beautiful in its simplicity and made her wonder if she'd ever meet anyone who would long to truly place a ring on her finger and be all to her that the gesture implied.

She doubted it.

Knox had unwittingly tapped her one weakness with the ring he'd bought her as a prop—her desire to be wanted.

Other than those few woefully short years with her parents, Savannah had never been truly wanted. While she'd certainly stayed with a few good families during her stint in the foster-care system, most families had taken her in either for the compensation or to add an indentured servant to their household. Sometimes both. A live-in maid, a built-in baby-sitter. But no one had ever truly wanted her.

Savannah had made the mistake of letting that weakness impair her judgment once with Gib, but she'd never do it again. Rejection simply hurt too much and wasn't worth the risk. She'd learned to become self-reliant, to trust her instincts, and never to depend on another person for her happiness.

"Wow," Knox murmured as they were led down a wide hall and finally shown into their room.

Wow, indeed, Savannah thought as she gazed at the plush surroundings. The natural hardwood floors and thick white plaster walls were a continued theme throughout the house, creating a light and airy atmosphere. Heavy wooden beams decorated the high white ceilings, tying the wood and white decor together seamlessly.

A huge canopied bed draped with yards and yards of rich brocade hangings occupied a place of honor in the middle of one long wall. Coordinating pieces—a chest of drawers, dresser and a couple of nightstands—balanced the room perfectly. A dinette sat in one corner and a small arched fireplace accented with rich Mexican tile added another splash of color and warmth. Multicolored braided rugs were scattered about the room, adding more depth to the large space. Light streamed in through two enormous arched windows. It was a great room, very conducive to romance, Savannah thought.

A ribbon of unease threaded through her belly as she once again considered why she was here—and what she'd have to resist. Savannah glanced at the bed and, to her consternation, imagined Knox and her vibrating the impressive four-poster across the room, her hands shaped to Knox's perfectly formed ass as he plunged in and out of her. She imagined candlelight and rose petals and hot, frantic bodies tangled amid the scented sheets. Savannah drew in a shuddering breath as dread and need coalesced into a fireball in her belly.

Knox cased the room, checked out the closet and adjoining bath. He whistled. "Hey, come check out the tub."

Given her wayward imagination, Savannah didn't think that would be wise. Visions of Knox wet and naked and needy weren't particularly helpful to her cause.

"So," Knox said as he returned from admiring the bath. "Which side of the bed do you want?"

Savannah blinked, forced a wry smile. "I think the question is which part of the floor do you want?"

Knox glanced at the gleaming hardwood and absently scratched his temple. He wore an endearing smile. "Do I have a prayer of winning this argument?"

"No." Savannah hated to be such a prude, but having to sleep next to him would be sheer and utter torture. Simply being in the same room with him would be agonizing enough. Savannah grimly suspected that were they to share that bed, she'd inexplicably gravitate toward him. Toward his marvelous ass. Considering he didn't reciprocate this unholy attraction, she wasn't about to risk embarrassing herself and him.

He sighed. "As the lady wishes. I suppose we should head to the common room for the Welcome Brunch."

Savannah nodded. Without further comment, the two of them exited the room and, with Knox's hand at her elbow, they made their way down a long wide hall back to the foyer and then into what had been dubbed the common room. A long table piled with food sat off to the side of the enormous room and little sofas and armchairs were grouped together to encourage idle chitchat. Savannah's stomach issued a hungry growl, propelling her toward the food.

"Hungry, are you?" Knox queried.

"Ravenous."

"I offered to share my peanuts with you," he reminded teasingly.

Savannah grunted. "I wasn't about to partake of your ill-gotten gains."

Knox chuckled, a deep silky baritone that made her very insides quiver. Jeez, the man had cornered the market when it came to sex appeal. It was the same sort of intimate laugh she assumed he'd share with a lover. Something warm and quivery snaked through her at the thought.

"I simply flirted a little, Savannah. It's not like I

raped and pillaged. Honestly, have you not ever batted your lashes and tried to get out of a speeding ticket?''

''No,'' she lied as she selected a wedge of cheese and a few crackers.

He chuckled again. ''Liar.''

''That's different,'' she said simply for the sake of disagreeing with him, which she did a lot. ''And it's Barbie, you idiot. Do you want to blow our cover from the get-go?''

''Whatever.'' He paused. ''Oh, look, our host and hostess have arrived.''

Savannah turned and her gaze landed on an older couple—early to middle fifties, she guessed. Bare feet peeked from beneath the hems of their long white robes. The woman wore her completely silver hair in a long flowing style that slithered over her shoulders and stopped at the small of her back. Silver charms glittered from her wrists and a large, smooth lavender stone lay suspended between her breasts via a worn leather cord. This woman seemed to embody everything their glossy pamphlet proclaimed. Serenity, harmony and all those other adverbs that had been touted in the trendy brochure.

As for the man, a calm strength seemed to hover about him as well. He appeared relaxed yet confident, as though he was the only stud for his mare. A niggle of doubt surfaced as Savannah studied the two. Could the art of tantric sex really be all this couple claimed it was? Quite honestly, it seemed impossible to Savannah, but for the first time since she'd accepted that she'd be working on this story with Knox, Savannah wondered if she'd been too hasty in forming her opinions.

The man smiled. "Welcome. I'm Dr. Edgar Shea and this is my lovely wife and life partner, Dr. Rupali Shea. We're so glad that you're here." He paused. "Some of you are here as a result of frustration, some of you are here as a result of your partner's prodding, and some of you are here because you're simply curious." His grin made an encore appearance. "Regardless of why you are here, we're exceedingly glad and are looking forward to teaching you everything we've learned about the art of tantric lovemaking. What we will teach you, what we'll freely share and will graphically demonstrate for your benefit, will change your lives…if you are open to the possibilities."

"At the beginning of each session," Rupali began, "we like to do a little preliminary test, to see for ourselves just how much ground we need to cover, to see which couples will require one-on-one instruction." She paused and smiled to the room at large. "Now don't look frightened. It's a simple test. But first we'll introduce ourselves and share our inadequacies. No embarrassment, no boundaries," she said. "Only truth healing."

Savannah and Knox shared a look of dread. She almost felt sorry for him, but quickly squelched the sentiment. This was a hell of his own making. He could burn with humiliation for all she cared. The couples around them looked as miserable as she and Knox and that made Savannah feel marginally better. As she listened, one man admitted chronic masturbation as his problem. There were a couple of other women delegated to the frigid-and-couldn't-reach-climax list, and even more men who embarrassingly mumbled impotency as their major handicap.

Rupali beamed at them when they were finished. "Now, for the test." She paused again, garnering everyone's attention with the heavy silence. She steepled her fingers beneath her chin. "Do any of you know what the most intimate act between lovers is?" she asked. "I'm sure that all of you are thinking about intercourse, or possibly oral sex…but you'd be wrong. It's kissing. Kissing requires more intimacy than any other facet of lovemaking. And that will be your test. You will embrace your partner and kiss, and Edgar and I will observe." She beamed at them. "See, that's easy enough."

Savannah heard several audible sighs resonate around the room, but hers and Knox's weren't among them. Kissing? Kiss Knox? In front of all these people? Right now? Knox seemed to be equally astounded, as he wore a frozen smile on his face. Panic ping-ponged through her abdomen, the blood rushed to her ears and every bit of moisture evaporated from Savannah's mouth.

Knox drew her to him, anchored his powerful arms about her back and waist. Longing ignited a fire of need in her belly. "Quit looking like she's just issued a death sentence," he hissed through a brittle smile. "We're supposed to be married, remember?"

Savannah made the mistake of looking up into his dark green eyes and felt need balloon below her belly button. An involuntary shiver danced up her spine and camped at her nape. Oh, hell. She was doomed. "Right," she said breathlessly.

"It's just a kiss," he said unsteadily. "We can handle it."

"On my count," Rupali trilled. "Three, two, one…kiss!"

With equal parts anticipation and anxiety, Savannah's eyes fluttered shut as Knox's warm lips descended to hers. The exquisite feel of his lips slanting over hers instantly overwhelmed her and she swallowed a deep sigh of satisfaction as his taste exploded on her tongue. He tasted like soda and peanuts and the faint flavor of salt clung to his lips. *And oh, mercy, could he kiss.* Savannah whimpered.

His kiss was firm yet soft and he suckled and fed at her mouth until Savannah's legs would scarcely support her. Oh, how many times had she dreamed of this? How many times had she imagined his mouth hungrily feeding at hers, his built-like-a-brick-wall body wrapped around hers? With a groan of pure delight, she pressed herself even more firmly against him and felt her nipples tingle and pearl. A similar experience commenced between her thighs as her feminine muscles dewed and tightened. Their tongues played a game of seek and retreat, and for every parlay, Savannah grew even more agitated, more needy. Knox tightened his hold around her, and she felt his hand slide from the small of her back and cup her bottom. Another blast of desire detonated, sending a bright flash of warmth zinging through her blood.

From the dimmest recesses of her mind, Savannah realized that the room had grown ominously quiet. She reluctantly dragged her lips away from Knox's and laid her head against his rapidly rising chest.

Edgar and Rupali Shea grinned broadly at them. Their eyes twinkled knowingly. "Clearly Knox and Barbie have passed our little test with glowing marks and no one-on-one instruction will be required."

A titter of amusement resonated around the room.

Savannah's cheeked blazed and it took every ounce of willpower not to melt out of Knox's embrace. She extricated herself with as much dignity as she could muster, considering she'd all but lashed her legs about his waist and begged him to pump her amid a room of confessed sexually challenged spectators.

She was pathetic. Utterly and completely pathetic. How on earth would she keep her attraction for him secret now? How? she mentally wailed.

Deciding the best defense was a better offense, Savannah leaned forward and whispered in his ear, "How about a little less tongue next time, Slick? I don't know what you were looking for back there, but I had my tonsils removed years ago.'' She patted his arm and calmly moved to pick up her plate.

Knox's dumbfounded expression was unequivocally priceless, igniting a glow of another sort.

4

A LITTLE LESS TONGUE? Knox wondered angrily. To his near slack-jawed astonishment, he'd never enjoyed kissing another woman more. He'd been so caught up in the melding of their mouths that all he could think about was how amazingly great she tasted, how wonderful her lips felt against his, and how much he longed to have her naked and flat on her back...

It was too much to contemplate. This was Savannah.

Savannah.

Admittedly, he'd always thought her gorgeous. The first time he'd met her, he'd felt the familiar tug of attraction. But then she'd blasted him with a frigid blue stare and she'd opened her sarcastic mouth, and he'd never entertained another amorous thought about her. That's why he'd chosen her for this trip, dammit, and yet the moment his lips had met hers he'd gone into a molecular meltdown. He'd wanted to show her how hot she made him, tell her how much he wanted her and...

And seconds after that mind-blowing kiss, Savannah had calmly offered criticism and then just as calmly returned to her lunch.

Knox was unequivocally stunned.

He'd been too bowled over by the impact of that kiss to even regulate his breathing, much less pretend that he hadn't been affected...and she'd not only been unaffected, but apparently had been so unmoved by the experience that she'd been able to remain detached and offer advice.

Heat spreading up his neck, Knox loaded his own plate from the buffet and inwardly fumed. He'd always considered himself an attentive lover, had always prided himself on learning what techniques turned a woman on, what would give her pleasure. He liked a vocal partner, one who didn't expect him to be a mind reader. He liked hearing what made a woman hot and enjoyed doing it for her even more. Throughout his career in the bedroom, he'd heard countless breathy pleas—*harder, faster, there* and *there,* and *almost* and *oh, God, there! Touch, suck, lick* and *nibble,* even *spank,* he'd heard it all.

But never—*never*—had he ever had a woman criticize his kiss.

His kiss had always been above reproach, with no room for improvement. Though most men considered kissing as a simple means to an end—Knox included, most of the time—he'd nonetheless made it a point to excel at that particular form of foreplay.

Ask any man and he'd tell you that, given the choice of having his tongue in a woman's mouth, or his hand in her panties, the panties would win hands down every time. That was the ultimate goal, after all, and men were linear thinkers. Point A to point B in the most economical fashion.

Sure they might get distracted by a creamy breast and pouty nipple, might even linger around a delightful belly button for a few seconds, but settling oneself firmly between a woman's thighs was always, without question, the ultimate goal.

While kissing Savannah a few moments ago—though the kiss couldn't have lasted more than thirty seconds—Knox's thoughts had immediately leaped ahead to the grand finale. He'd already imagined plunging dick first into the tight, wet heat of her body. Had been anticipating her own phenomenally cataclysmic release as well as his.

While she'd been critiquing his kiss.

Knox had never anticipated being attracted to her and had known that she wasn't attracted to him, had chosen her for that particular reason. But having the knowledge confirmed in such a humiliating fashion wasn't an easy pill to swallow. Particularly since he'd all but devoured her and had made such a horny ass out of himself. Jesus. After that lusty display, there couldn't be one shred of doubt in her mind about how he'd reacted to her. How hot he'd been for her.

All due to a simple kiss she hadn't even enjoyed.

Simmering with indignation once more, Knox cast a sidelong glance at the object of his present irritation. Savannah's cheeks were a little pink—obviously embarrassed by his zealous response to their "test"—but aside from that, she appeared completely composed. She absently nibbled a cracker, her perceptive gaze roaming around the room people-watching, presumably looking for fodder for their story.

Which was exactly what he should be doing, Knox realized with an angry start. He mentally snorted. Undoubtedly she was already forming an angle, had already thought of an intro to their piece. Well, he'd have the most input, thank you very much. This story had been his brainchild, and if there had been any way he could have done it without her, he would have. And he wished he could have. They'd scarcely begun this damned workshop and already he'd become too distracted by the supposedly *undistracting* female he'd brought with him.

How screwed up was that?

"I hope you don't plan to pout the entire afternoon," Savannah said with a sardonic smile. "Honestly, Knox, it was only a small criticism. Surely that enormous ego of yours can take one minor unflattering assessment."

Ignoring a surge of irritation, Knox mentally counted to three, then arranged his face into its typically amiable expression. "Pout?"

Her eyes narrowed, clearly seeing through his innocent look. "Yes, pout. You've been glowering at the room at large for the past five minutes. Jeez, I didn't mean to hurt your feelings.'' She neatly bit the end off a stalk of celery. Her lips twitched. "Frankly, I wasn't aware that you had any."

Ah...back to familiar ground. Knox forced a smile, affected a negligent shrug, though he longed to wrap his hands around her throat and throttle her. He'd learned to appreciate her acidic sarcasm, but right now he wasn't in the proper humor to applaud her clever witticisms. He ignored her last comment and decided a change of subject was in order.

"So, what's your initial impression of the Sheas?" Knox asked.

Savannah winced, wiped a bit of salad dressing from the corner of her luscious lips. "They're what I expected...but then again they're not." She paused consideringly. "I don't know. It'll take more than a welcome speech for me to make an accurate assessment."

"I didn't ask for an accurate assessment. I asked for an initial impression."

"There's a difference?"

He nodded. "Of course.".

"What is it?"

She had to be the most infuriating female he'd ever met. "Stop being difficult and answer the question."   .

Seemingly resigned, Savannah blew out a breath. "They were impressive, Knox," she admitted reluctantly. "If I was like these people, desperately looking for a way to better my relationship with a significant other, my husband, or simply needing a little show-and-tell to jump-start my sex life, I'd like them. They seemed genuine.''

Secretly he agreed. Hokey togas aside, the Sheas seemed to share some secret something. Something the rest of the room lacked, or wasn't privy to. Still... " 'Seemed' is the key word.''

"I know." Savannah discarded her empty plate and dusted her hands. "So what's next on the agenda?''

Knox stacked his empty plate on top of hers. "We pick up our registration packets.''

She nodded. "Then let's do it. I want a chance to go over everything before our first class starts.''

Still feeling a little put out, Knox followed Savannah from the large common room and into the hall where the registration table had been set up. Several couples had been equally eager to start and Knox recognized the one in front of them with a little wince of dread—the masturbator and his wife.

Savannah's steps slowed. "Is that who I think—''

"Yes, it is," Knox hissed through a false smile as the couple in question turned with bright grins to greet them.

"Hi," the wife enthused. "Knox and Barbie, right? We're the Cummings. I'm Marge and this is my husband, Chuck.'' With a roll of her eyes, she jabbed her husband in the side. "Jeez, Chuck, where are your manners? Shake Knox's hand.''

Knox felt his frozen smile falter and his gaze

dropped to Chuck's outstretched hand with a paralyzing dread.

Beside him, Savannah covered her mouth with her hand and quickly morphed a chuckle into a convincing cough. He'd kill her when this was over with, Knox decided. He'd simply wring her neck.

The silence lengthened past the comfortable and Knox was resignedly readying his hand for the shake when Marge chirped "Gotcha!" amid a stream of high-pitched staccato laughter. The laugh went on and on and had the effect of fingernails on a chalkboard.

Chuck, too, was caught up in a fit of hilarity. His beefy face turned beet-red and, wheezing laughter, he pointed at Knox. "Man, if you could have seen your face! Oh, Marge, that was priceless. Utterly priceless. The best one yet."

Marge's laughter tittered out and she wiped her streaming eyes. "It's a little joke we like to pull," she confided, as though this whole scene was perfectly normal. "Everyone knows Chuck's a chronic masturbator—hell, I had to pry his hand away from his groin during your kiss a little while ago—so no one ever wants to shake his hand. *Ever,*" she added meaningfully. "I mean, who would, knowing where it's been, right?" She and Chuck shared a secret smile. "So we like to pull a little prank with it. We've gotten a variety of reactions, but yours was by far the best we've seen in a long time. You looked like he'd whipped out his poor overworked penis and asked you to shake it.''

Marge and Chuck dissolved into fits of whooping laughter once more.

Savannah, of course, was observing the whole scenario as he would expect—tickled to death at his expense. Her pale blue eyes glittered with barely restrained laughter. Knox could tell she was on the verge of pulling a Marge and he cast her one long, pointed look to dissuade her. Hadn't she ever heard of loyalty? She was supposed to be his wife, dammit, and should be outraged on his behalf. Not quivering with amusement over his immense discomfort.

Knox decided this was the point where he was supposed to laugh and managed to push a weak little ha-ha from his throat. It was exceedingly difficult, considering he longed to plant his fist through a wall. Or possibly Chuck's face.

''FYI, he's left-handed,'' Marge shared with another maddening little smile. ''You could have shaken it without a thing to worry about.''

Knox forced his lips into a smile. Thankfully, Marge and Chuck's turn at the registration table came, sparing him a reply.

''Well,'' Savannah whispered through her curling lips, ''that was certainly interesting.''

Knox felt a muscle jump in his jaw. ''You think?''

''Funny, too.''

''I'm glad you were amused,'' Knox ground out.

''Marge was right,'' she went on to his supreme

annoyance. She rocked back on her heels. "The look on your face *was* priceless. I wish I'd had a camera."

Knox smirked. "You're really enjoying this, aren't you, Savannah?"

She aimed a smugly beautiful smile in his direction, clasped her hands behind her back and batted her lashes shamelessly. "Yes. Yes, I am." She sighed. "After what you pulled with Chapman, can you really blame me?"

Knox exhaled wearily. He supposed not, and reluctantly admitted as much. "Still," he told her. "Gloating does not become you. Enough already, Savannah. We've got a job to do," he reminded her pointedly, as much for his own benefit as hers. Focus, Knox told himself. The big picture. He needed to push the kiss and the masturbator encounter out of his mind and keep the ultimate goal in sight—the story.

"I know that," she snapped, clearly perturbed at the reminder. "Believe me, that's the only reason I'm here—for the story. Let's just register and go back to our room. I want to prepare for this class." She chuckled darkly. "And let's pray there aren't any more surprise tests."

Damn right, Knox thought. At the moment, he wasn't up for another failing grade from "Barbie."

AS SOON AS THEY RETURNED to their room, Savannah made a beeline for the bathroom. She needed a few moments alone—just a few precious seconds away from Knox's distracting company to regroup and pull herself together. Once behind the closed door, she blew out a pent-up breath, then ran the tap and splashed cold water on her face. It felt cool and refreshing and helped alleviate some of the tension tightening her neck and shoulders.

Her muscles had atrophied with stress after The Kiss.

Sure, she'd managed to put on a good enough show, had forced herself to appear cool and unaffected when the truth of the matter had been that Knox's kiss had all but melted her bones. When his talented mouth had touched hers…

Mercy.

Remembered heat sent a coil of longing swirling through the pit of her belly. Her nipples tightened and a familiar but woefully missed warmth weighted her core.

She'd known—hadn't she?—that he would be utterly amazing. Her every instinct had told her so, just as every instinct had warned her against him. She'd managed to undermine his self-confidence this time, managed to miraculously pull off a grand performance, but he'd undoubtedly see through her if anything like that happened between them again.

Though she hadn't yet had a chance to go through the curriculum, Savannah nonetheless knew that the kiss was just the beginning of what the workshop would entail. She and Knox would be called upon to do much more than kiss. The success of the Sheas' workshop depended upon it.

She wished that she and Knox could keep up the ruse without having to participate physically in class, and the wishing, she knew, was an act of futility. They would have to participate to some extent in class, otherwise they'd call attention to themselves, or, worse still, would lead the Sheas to believe they needed more intensive therapy.

Savannah shuddered. Neither scenario inspired confidence.

Irritation rose. Savannah ground her teeth and resisted the urge to beat her head against the door. This was precisely why she didn't want to be here, she inwardly fumed. Savannah knew her limits, knew her shortcomings and knew what sort of effect Knox Webber had on her libido. Attending a sex workshop with him was like waving a joint in front of a pothead.

Knox would be addictive to her and the addiction could only lead to heartache—hers.

She simply wouldn't allow it.

Chapman had forced her hand by making her attend. Despite her misgivings, Savannah would do her job and write a great story—and she'd do all that the task entailed, including being an objective participant in this godforsaken workshop—she was a professional, after all. But she would not let it become personal.

She wouldn't.

Seeing as sex was about as personal as it got, Savannah wasn't exactly sure what her heartfelt affirmation meant, but it made her feel better and she'd use any means available to shore up her waning confidence.

A tentative knock sounded at the door, startling her.

"Savannah...you all right in there?"

"Y-yes, of course." Savannah flushed the commode for appearance's sake, drew in a deep bolstering breath and smoothed her hair behind her ears.

"I, uh, wouldn't bother you, but I need to change and, frankly, I've gotta go."

Frowning, Savannah opened the door. "Change?" she asked. "Change for what?"

Knox had tossed a long white garment over his shoulder. It looked suspiciously like the same sort of costume the Sheas wore.

"For class," he told her. "We have to wear a *kurta*. I'm going to feel like a complete moron," he confided with an endearing, self-conscious smile, "but they're mandatory. I laid yours on the bed."

Good grief, Savannah thought, wondering what other little surprises would be in store for this weekend. She sighed heavily and massaged the bridge of her nose. "A *what?*"

"A *kurta*. It's an Indian gown."

Savannah eyed the getup warily. She crossed her arms over her chest. "You've got to be kidding."

"Nope...and it gets worse."

The hesitation in Knox's voice alerted her more than the actual words he'd said. "Worse?"

He winced regretfully. "Yeah—no undergarments. And no shoes."

Savannah blinked, flabbergasted. She was supposed to walk around naked under a toga? "No undergarments?" she repeated blankly, certain that she'd misunderstood him.

He tunneled his fingers through his hair, mussing up the wavy brown locks. "Yeah, I'm afraid so. It's to promote chakra healing, and, of course, the symbolic message of no boundaries."

And easy access, Savannah thought, for those graphic hands-on demonstrations. Her mouth parched and dread ballooned in her chest.

"Uh, if you're finished in there..." Knox reminded her.

Belatedly Savannah realized she still stood in the threshold of the bathroom. "Oh, sure. Sorry," she mumbled, hastily moving out of his way.

"I've had a quick look through the itinerary for the weekend," Knox called through the door. "After you get dressed, you might want to flip through it."

"I plan to," Savannah murmured absently as she picked up the long, white gown. The cool, soft cotton material smelled of fresh air. It had probably been line-dried, Savannah decided, not tossed into an industrial-sized appliance. Still, knowing that she'd be walking around buck naked underneath the almost see-through fabric quickly dispelled any pleasant musings.

Oh, hell. Knox would be out of the bathroom soon, so unless she wanted to do a little striptease for him, she'd best change before he came out. Savannah hurriedly removed her shoes, pantsuit, bra and undies, then picked up the gown and pulled it over her head. The fabric settled on her shoulders lightly, whispered over her body and came to rest just above her ankles. It felt surprisingly…good. Wicked even, if she were honest. Something about the way the garment caressed her body made her feel beautiful, free and sexy. She particularly liked the way the material felt against her bare breasts and rump.

"Are you dressed yet?" Knox called.

Savannah scrambled up onto the bed, put her back against the headboard and settled a pillow over her lap. She grabbed the handbook and made herself look studious and calm. It took a tremendous amount of effort.

"Uh…yeah," she finally managed.

Knox exited the bathroom. He'd obviously brushed his hair, as the brown waves were once more smoothed back into place. His lips were curled into an almost bashful, self-deprecating grin and those incredibly lean cheeks were washed in an uncharacteristic pink. He'd folded his clothes and had tucked them up under his arm. A curious emotion swelled in Savannah's chest.

Knox gestured to the *kurta*. "I don't think that I've

ever felt more emasculated in my life. If I'd known that wearing a damned dress with no drawers on underneath would be a mandatory part of this workshop, I simply would have said to hell with the story and found something else to write about.''

Well, Savannah thought, as every drop of moisture evaporated from her mouth, he might feel emasculated, but he definitely didn't *look* emasculated.

In fact, if he looked any less emasculated, he'd be X-rated. She could clearly see through the fabric, and the impressive bulge beneath indicated that Knox Webber was, without question, the most unemasculated man she'd ever seen—and he wasn't even hard. Fascinated, she swallowed. That was just…him. Just…there. All him.

Sweet heaven.

Every cell in her body was hammeringly aware that less than five feet from where she sat stood the most incredibly sexy, most generously endowed man she'd ever seen in her life. She instantly imagined him out of the *kurta* and sprawled on the bed next to her. Her blood thickened and desire sparked other fantasies, so she took her wicked illusion to the next level and imagined herself sinking slowly onto the hot, hard length of him. Sweet mother of heaven…

Savannah bit her lip, fully engrossed in the picture her wayward imagination had conjured. Up until now she'd always been preoccupied with his ass—he had an amazing ass, after all—but Savannah grimly suspected that fixation had just been replaced with another. Honestly, how did he make all of that fit in—

"What about you? Do you feel ridiculous?" Knox asked.

Savannah blinked drunkenly and then, feeling stupid and ashamed, recovered the next instant. "Er, yes. Yes, I do."

Knox paused to look at her. A line emerged between his brows. "You're acting weird. Are you sure you're all right?"

"Yeah, I'm fine." She manufactured a smile and thumped the booklet that lay in her lap. "Just thinking about some of the names for these classes."

Seemingly satisfied, Knox smiled knowingly. "You mean like *Love His Lingam, Rejuvenate His Root?*"

Savannah laughed. "Yeah. And *Sacred Goddess Stimulation.*"

Thank God those classes would come later, Savannah thought. They got to learn all about their chakras first with *Beginning Tantra, Energetic Healing.*

"So, what do you say?" Knox asked. "Ready to go get your chakras aligned?"

Savannah heaved a put-upon sigh. "Honestly, Knox. This isn't like the front end of your car. You're not getting anything aligned. Haven't you done your homework? You're getting unblocked." Savannah slid from the bed and gathered her things.

"Getting what unblocked?"

A sly smile curled her lips. "Well, for starters, your ass."

5

FOLLOWING SAVANNAH out the door, Knox involuntarily tightened the orifice in question. *"What?"*

"For someone who was so determined to do this story—*had* to do this particular story," she emphasized sarcastically, "it would seem that you would have put a little more research into the project."

"I did my research," Knox insisted with a sardonic smile. "But I didn't come across anything that suggested tantra partners began foreplay with an enema."

Savannah chuckled darkly. "Who said anything about an enema?"

"Well, how else—" Knox drew up short as realization dawned. His ass instantly clenched in horror.

Oh, hell.

Catching his appalled expression, Savannah's pale blue eyes sparkled with amusement. That sinfully beautiful mouth of hers curved ever so slightly with mockery. "Aha. Light dawns on marble head."

Knox swallowed and continued to follow her down the hall. He'd rather be eviscerated with a rusty blade than even think about anal sex, much less discuss the loathsome subject with Savannah. He didn't need to get unblocked, thank you very much, and after a moment told her so. Forcibly.

She winced, clearly enjoying his discomfort. "Don't worry, Knox, I was kidding about the visit to the back door. But I have to say, you have one glaring characteristic of a man who needs to have his root chakra unblocked."

A muscle worked in his jaw. Knox knew better than to ask, but found himself forming the question anyway. "Really? And what characteristic would that be?"

"You're a tight-ass. I think I've pointed that out to you before."

Knox smirked. "Cute."

He held open the heavy front door and allowed her to pass. Their first class was on the south lawn in the outdoor classroom. Butterflies and bumblebees flitted from flower to flower through the Sheas' eclectic garden, Knox noticed as he and Savannah made their way across the lush lawn. Grass pushed between his toes, bringing a reluctant grin to his lips. It had been a long time since he'd been barefoot in the grass.

A peek at Savannah confirmed that she was enjoying the sensation as well. A small smiled tilted her lips and she'd turned her face toward the kiss of the sun. A light breeze ruffled her black bed-head locks and that same breeze molded the white, all-but-see-through *kurta* to her small, womanly form.

It was at this point that Knox became hopelessly distracted.

Naturally, over the course of Savannah's career at the *Phoenix,* Knox had observed her body and noted its perfection. He was a man, after all, and men—being men—tended to notice such details.

But noticing and really appreciating were two completely different things.

Knox's gaze roamed leisurely over her body and, much to his helpless chagrin, his visual perusal ignited a spark of heat in his loins.

The delicate fabric lay plastered against the unbound globes of her breasts, and the rosy hue of her nipples shadowed through the clinging material. Knox could easily discern the flat belly, the sweetly curving swell of her hips and the black triangle of curls nestled at the apex of her thighs.

She was beautiful. Utterly and completely beautiful and...

And feeling his dick begin to swell for sport, Knox mentally swore and made a determined effort to direct his lust-ridden brain toward a more productive line of thought—like his story. With that idea in mind, he studied his surroundings.

Picnic tables, some already occupied with couples, were arranged in a large circle beneath a huge whitewashed octagon canopy. Crystals of various sizes and shapes dripped like icicles from the perimeter of the canopy, sending rainbows of colorful reflected light dancing through the air. The tinkling tones of wind chimes sounded, adding another element to the mystical environment. A white silk chaise sat upon a raised dais in the center of the outdoor room. Who knew what sort of depraved acts had been committed upon that little bench, Knox thought with a grim smile.

"Where should we sit?" Savannah asked as she surveyed the circle of tables.

"Somewhere in the middle," Knox told her. "If we sit in front, we'll look eager and too easy to snag for demonstrations. If we sit in the back, they'll think we're bashful and will want to draw us in and make us participate." He guided her toward an appropriate table.

Savannah grinned. "Why do I feel like this is the voice of experience and not a fabricated load of BS?"

"Because it is. I honed the skill in grade school."

With a roll of her eyes, Savannah sat down. "Sounds like you were trying to figure out a way to do the least amount of work possible."

Knox returned her grin and attempted to sit down next to her. He wasn't used to navigating in a dress and almost toppled chin first into the picnic table when the hem of the *kurta* caught the seat. He scowled, smoothing the damned gown back into place. "That was one of the perks," he finally said. "Be sure and take good notes. I always copied someone else's."

She gave him a droll glare. "I'm sure you did."

Actually, he hadn't. He'd only been trying to needle her. What did she think? That he'd been able to sail through an Ivy League school on nothing but his parents' money and his charming personality? And she had the nerve to think him a snob?

She'd never said it, of course. Just like none of his other co-workers had ever said it. But Knox knew they were laboring under the mistaken assumption that his wealthy background had afforded him his present career and, moreover, that his being talented could have nothing to do with it.

Knox smothered a bitter laugh. Let them think what they would. Screw 'em. He didn't care. In fact, he purposely invested a great deal of time making sure that no one—least of all any of those co-workers at the paper—knew just how much he longed to be respected for his work, rather than simply tolerated with virulent envy.

Between his condescending co-workers and equally condescending parents, Knox was doubly determined to succeed.

For reasons that escaped him, Savannah's opinion, in particular, annoyed the hell out of him. But what did he expect? That after spending one day with him, she'd see him any differently than she always had? That his character would have suddenly jumped up a notch in her esteemed estimation? Not likely. And he didn't care, dammit. He *did not* care. When he made it, when he proved himself, she'd be just like everyone else—eating crow.

Curiously, the thought didn't inspire the smug satisfaction Knox anticipated and, instead left him feeling small and petty. He shrugged the sensation aside and focused instead on the Sheas as they finally moved onto the dais.

"Welcome to your first class," Edgar began. "The title of this lesson is *Beginning Tantra/Energetic Healing.* We have much ground to cover over the course of this weekend and everything we teach you will be built upon these basic tantric principles, so please have your pad and pencil poised and be ready to learn."

"Before we begin," Rupali said to the class at large, "there are a few things we must cover." She steepled her fingers beneath her chin, the picture of glowing serenity. "I'm sure you are all wondering why you've been asked to wear the *kurta* and remove your shoes. Let me address the *kurta* first. The *kurta* denotes purity, helps promote chakra healing and enables us all to remove psychological boundaries. At times, our clothes can be our armor against our sensual selves." Her keen gaze landed pointedly on a few people. Savannah, too, Knox noticed with mild surprise. "We'll have no armor here. Only truth and healing." She paused. "As for not wearing shoes, we need to be grounded to Mother Earth, to let her energy flow up through our feet and connect us once more with the force of all that's natural, that's pure. Curl your toes in the grass—let it massage your feet," she instructed. "Isn't it nice? Can you feel

Mother Earth's power?'' she asked, smiling. ''If not, you will by the end of this clinic, I promise you. All of you will leave here with a new sense of energy, of purpose, of happiness.''

''That's a mighty big promise,'' Savannah whispered from the side of her mouth.

Knox nodded. ''Yeah, but it's what she didn't promise that's wise. She didn't promise impotent men erections, and she didn't promise you frigid-unable-to-climax types an orgasm.''

''You're right,'' she quietly agreed. ''It's inferred, but not stated. Smart move. Very crafty.''

''Are there any questions so far?'' Rupali wanted to know. ''If not, then we'll move on to the next item on the agenda before we officially begin class. In order to insure that you fully understand and appreciate what sort of sexual gratification tantra can add to your sex lives, you need to understand what was lacking in the first place, and you need to be able to instantly discern the vast difference between the lovers you officially are today and the new lovers you will become. What I'm about to ask of you will be exceedingly difficult, but it's simply crucial to the success of your experience—you must abstain from physical intercourse until the end of the workshop.''

A chorus of shocked gasps and giggles echoed under the pavilion.

''It's crucial,'' she repeated firmly. ''Men, through tantra we're going to teach you the most effective way to bring your lover pleasure. We're going to teach you to worship your goddess. The techniques you will learn will enable you to prolong your own inner release as well as hers.''

"Likewise ladies," she continued, "we will teach you the most effective way to worship your man, to massage and heal, and bring pleasure beyond anything he's ever experienced before. We want you to make love, want to encourage you to grow spiritually as well as sexually with your partners. But there are lessons to be learned first." She laughed. "Lessons that will have you writhing with pleasure and begging for the most carnal form of release. But you can't have it…yet. Consummation will occur on Sunday night and not a moment before. Does everyone agree to this rule?"

After a few reluctant nods and one gentle but firm admonishment to Chuck, who'd been busy throughout her speech, Rupali finally concluded, and Edgar stood once more.

He clapped his hands together. "Okay, let's begin," he said.

While Edgar began a brief summary of each of the chakras, Knox's thoughts still lingered over Rupali's revelation—no consummation until Sunday. He couldn't begin to imagine why this was relevant to him as he and Savannah weren't going to be consummating anything. Still…

Just knowing that they were going to have to participate in everything—learn all of the supposed pleasure-enhancing techniques—up until that point and then miss the grand finale was heartily depressing. Unreasonable, he knew. The whole point of bringing Savannah along was to remain asexual about the entire concept, to remain focused on the story. The nudge was still there, powerful as ever.

Jeez. He was pathetic. Obviously, he was so preoccupied with his pecker that being denied even mythological sex irritated him. Knox cast a sidelong glance at his companion and felt his lips twitch with wry humor. If she had any inkling of the direction of his thoughts right now, she'd undoubtedly pull a Lorena Bobbitt and permanently extinguish his "wand of light" like she'd so lethally threatened before.

So, he could either keep this one-sided attraction to himself—which unquestionably would be the sanest and most healthy thing he could do—or he could work on her until it was no longer one-sided.

With luck, the weekend would be over before he came to a clear decision.

"DOES ANYONE KNOW what the word *tantra* means?" Edgar asked. "It means to weave, or extend."

Right, Savannah thought. She'd known the answer, but couldn't make her sluggish brain form the required definition—she was too busy mourning the loss of the great spiritual sex she'd never intended to have in the first place.

And not just any sex.

Sex with Knox.

Savannah knew she shouldn't feel like wailing with frustration. Shouldn't feel like whimpering with regret. But she did. He'd been sitting beside her for the past hour, and her palm had literally itched to reach over to shape her hand to the oh-so-clearly defined length of him. She wanted to stroke him, to feel him grow in her hand, grow inside her. Which was ludicrous. Knox had admitted that the sole reason he'd asked her to attend this sex workshop was because she happened to be the only woman he could bring along that he *wouldn't* want to sleep with. He'd admitted that he didn't find her the least bit attractive.

And that was a good thing, dammit. She didn't want him to be attracted to her. It would be nothing short of ruinous. She'd already dated a pretty prep-school playboy and he'd given her the old heave-ho the minute his parents had squawked their disapproval. As far as the Lyleses had been concerned, Savannah had been foster-care trash, not worthy of their precious pedigreed son.

There were a gazillion reasons why she shouldn't have hot, sweaty phenomenal sex with Knox. Savannah's insides grew warm and muddled at the mere implication of the act. Still, he was like Gib, he had a love-'em-and-leave-'em reputation, he was a co-worker... The list went on and on.

Yet none of them—or the combined total—could hold a candle to the ferocity of the attraction.

Every part of him that was male drew every part

her that was female. She yearned for him. Longed to
have those big beautiful hands of his shaped around
her breasts. That talented mouth tasting every mole,
every freckle, everywhere that was white and everywhere that was pink.

And she wanted to touch him as well, wanted to
slide her fingers over each and every perfectly
formed sinew. Wanted to feel that powerful body un-
leashed with passion and, ultimately, sated with release. She sighed.

She just wanted.

Savannah swallowed another frustrated wail.
She'd kept her distance, hadn't she? She'd even
made herself dislike him, all in an effort to avoid this
very predicament. All of that hard work for this beautiful mess.

Even if the talk of sex finally sparked some latent
interest in him, he'd never be so pathetically unpro-
fessional as to act upon it. For reasons Savannah
didn't understand, this particular story was incredibly
important to him. He'd coerced her into coming, after
all. He'd never jeopardize the story, regardless of
how much he might like to overthrow his traditional
tastes and take her for a quick tumble between the
sheets.

So she needed to put the whole idea out of her
mind. She'd forget that damned kiss and pray they
wouldn't have to participate in that madness again.
She'd ignore the enormous penis draped across his

thigh beneath that *kurta* and her own beaded nipples and moist sex and…

And, Savannah realized with mounting frustration, she'd undoubtedly end up masturbating the entire weekend, just like poor oversexed Chuck.

"Hey," Knox said as he gently nudged her in the side. "I thought I told you to take notes. You stopped at the genital chakra."

That seemed appropriate, Savannah thought. "Sorry," she mumbled.

"Don't worry about it. We've got to go over all of it and work on unblocking as many chakras as we can tonight for homework. At the end of this lesson we move on to building trust between partners and the art of erotic massage." Knox waggled his brows suggestively. "They have scented massage oil in the gift shop."

Six and a half feet of gloriously oiled, aroused male loomed in her mind's eye. "Great," she managed to deadpan. "You can rub it all over yourself."

Shaking his head, Knox tsked under his breath. "Now what could we possibly learn from that? How can we do this story justice without at least trying some of the techniques?"

She couldn't fault his reasoning, though that was her first impulse. Still, if they tried one, she'd want to try them all. Which meant it would be best to forgo the whole lot. "I suppose you should have thought of that before you hauled me to a sex workshop."

"Who said anything about having sex? It's just a massage. Are you planning on giving this story anything but your best objective opinion?"

Savannah bristled. "Of course not."

"Then it's a no-brainer," he said with a negligent shrug. "Tell you what, I'll go you one better and do you first. How does that sound?"

Like torture, Savannah thought. Delicious torture, but torture all the same. "Whatever." She gestured toward the Sheas. "They're about to conclude the lesson. Shut up and pay attention."

"In a few moments we'll take a short break, and then we'll move on to part one of our erotic massage lesson," Edgar said. "Before we stop, however, let's take a moment to quietly reflect and connect with our lovers."

Oh, hell, Savannah thought with a premonition of dread. That didn't sound good.

"Everyone please stand," Rupali instructed. "For some, this is a very difficult exercise, but Edgar and I didn't promise that this weekend would be easy. The level of intimacy we want our students to achieve requires that fears and inadequacies be set aside, that the true self be revealed."

Savannah resisted the urge to squirm. It was sounding worse.

"One of the simplest ways to do that is to maintain eye contact, to search your partner's eyes and reveal past hurts, regrets, happiness and love." Rupali paused and gauged the room's reaction to her words.

"In time, you will be able to look into your partner's eyes and see your *Imago,* or mirror image, reflected back at you. While you might be uncomfortable now, the longer you practice tantra, the more you strive for a more spiritual union, you will eventually learn to prize this very special connection."

Edgar set the timer on his watch. "Men, pull your women to you, so that their heart beats against your chest. So that you can feel the steady rhythm of her life force thumping against you."

Knox, damn him, didn't appear the least bit annoyed or uncomfortable by this new test as, smiling, he did as Edgar instructed and pulled her firmly up against the hard wall of his magnificent chest.

With a decidedly sick smile, Savannah's own heart threatened to pound right through her ribcage. In addition to feeling Knox's heartbeat, she felt the telltale ridge of his "wand of light" against her belly button and, to her eternal chagrin, her "sacred space" swiftly grew warm and wet. If he'd branded her with the damned thing, she couldn't have felt it more.

"Now, women, wrap your arms about your man's waist. Wrap him in your love. Let him see it." Edgar chuckled. "It's true men are visual creatures. They have to see to believe. Make him *believe.*"

"For the next ninety seconds," Rupali said, "we're going to stand together and gaze into each other's eyes. Blink if you must, but try to maintain eye contact. Don't look away and do not speak. Say it with your eyes, use your brow chakra to learn your lover's secrets. You may begin...now.''

Feeling utterly and completely ridiculous, not to mention incredibly uncomfortable, Savannah did as Rupali said and looked up into Knox's twinkling green eyes. Commiserating laughter lurked in that verdant gaze, Savannah noticed to her marginal relief. She quelled the desire to squirm. Her breasts had already tightened into hard little buds and if she moved as she wished to, she might not be able to stop. Pathetic, but true.

Knox's eyes were heavy lidded, with long, curling lashes. The green was pure, just flecked with lighter and darker hues, but no shades of brown commonly found in a color as dark as his. Some of the humor faded from his gaze and another indiscernible emotion took its place. Something heavy and intense and altogether sexy. Savannah pulled in an unsteady breath. She thought she saw a reciprocating heat, but knew that couldn't be the case. Simply wishful thinking on her part.

Still, the longer the stare went on—Jesus, who would have thought that a minute and a half would seem like a lifetime?—the more aroused she became. Her limbs had grown heavy and she'd transferred some of the weight by leaning more closely into him. She had the almost overpowering urge to lower her gaze to his lips, then let her own mouth follow that path.

If she lived to be one hundred, she didn't think she'd ever want to kiss a man more.

The desire was completely out of the realm of her limited experience. The pressing need built and built until the longing and weight of that heady stare seemed almost unbearable. Savannah felt herself sagging closer and closer to him and, though she knew better, she simply didn't possess the strength to stop it. If this didn't end soon, she'd—

"Time's up," Edgar called, and the group underneath the pavilion heaved a collective sigh. "Now kiss your lover, then we'll adjourn for a break."

A relief of another sort gripped Savannah and she eagerly met Knox's mouth as it descended hungrily to hers. The unmistakable—enormous—length of him nudged her navel and, rather than be alarmed, which would have been the intelligent reaction, Savannah merely smiled against his mouth and thought, *Oh, thank God, I'm not the only one, after all.*

Knox Webber could claim he wasn't attracted to her, but she'd just been presented with some hard evidence that proved otherwise.

Granted, men awoke with a hard-on, and could typically get it up for just about any woman. His reaction was likely due to part of the intense lesson and all the talk of genital chakras, but for this moment—*just this one*—she would pretend otherwise. Savannah generally avoided lying to herself at all costs, but surely this one little fib couldn't hurt. Right?

It's not like she'd ever be so cork-brained as to delude herself into thinking that he felt anything but mild disdain toward her. She may have been able to turn on his "wand of light," but when it came to generating any real interest, the lights were off and no one was home.

6

KNOX STARED DOWN into Savannah's ice-blue gaze
and the effect of that cool stare left him anything but
chilly. The first fifteen to twenty seconds of their so-
called exercise she'd been adorably shy, utterly miserable and obviously so far out of her comfort zone
he'd found himself smiling to reassure her.

Knox was a man who always questioned everything—that insatiable curiosity had prompted his career choice. Savannah's reaction to this particular test
raised many questions, the most pressing of which
was, who or what had happened to her to make her
so damned distrustful? Because something definitely
had.

At some point in her life, or perhaps repeatedly,
she'd been deeply hurt. Betrayed. The knowledge
made his mind momentarily go black with rage and
the unreasonable urge to right old wrongs for her,
heal old hurts.

How could he have been so blind? He could see
the truth now, hovering beneath the bravado, beneath
the sarcasm, and he wondered again how he'd ever
missed it in the first place. Knox mentally snorted.

Hell, he knew how. She'd never let him close enough. Never let anyone close enough, for that matter.

To be honest, Knox hadn't been thrilled with the prospect of another test, but when Edgar had instructed them to wrap their arms about their woman, Knox had grown decidedly more enthusiastic about the lesson. He'd watched her emotions flash like neon signs through her eyes and the one that finally managed to completely undo him was passion.

Those cool blue eyes had rapidly warmed until they glowed like a blue flame. A resulting heat swept him from the top of his head to the tips of his bare toes. His heart had begun to pound, sending the blood that much faster to his throbbing groin. The hairs on his arms prickled and the nudge he normally associated with work began an insistent jab.

As the seconds ticked by, Savannah gravitated closer and closer to him until he could feel her budded nipples against his chest. Could feel the rhythmic beating of her heart as the Sheas had instructed. Feeling that rapid, steady beat did have a curious effect on him, Knox conceded. He'd never thought much about his heart, other than being aware that it pumped his blood, but something about feeling hers made him want to pull an Alfalfa, cancel his membership in the He-Man-Woman-Hater's Club and beat his chest and roar. He'd made her heart pound. Him. What a turn-on.

Knowing that she was naked underneath that

gown, that nothing more than a thin wisp of cotton separated his skin from hers tortured him, made his hands itch to feel her through the fabric. Knox pulled in a shaky breath and quelled the almost overwhelming urge to back her onto the picnic table, hike up that *kurta* and bury himself into the slick velvet heat of her body. Piston in and out of her until their simultaneous cries of release rent the air and he spilled his seed deep into the tight glove of her body.

Clearly he'd lost his mind, to be having such thoughts about Savannah. They were here to do a job, nothing more, and yet he'd give everything he owned right now just to kiss her. Just to taste her. Just one small—

"Time's up," Edgar called. "Now kiss your lover and we'll adjourn for a break."

Kiss your lover...

Knox groaned with giddy relief and quickly lowered his mouth to hers. To his immense delight, Savannah met him halfway and her mouth clung to his, fed greedily until nothing existed but the feel of her against him, the exquisite taste of her on his tongue.

What the kiss lacked in finesse it more than made up for with passion. She lashed her arms about his neck and all but crawled up his body to get closer, ran her hands all over him, cupped his ass and growled her approval right into his mouth. She eagerly explored his mouth, slid her tongue around his, tasted the fleshy part of his lips. She nibbled and sucked, and it occurred to Knox that, at some point in the near future, he'd like to have her do the same thing to his rod. She wriggled and writhed, alternately sighed and purred with pleasure and each little note of praise caused *both* of his heads to swell, particularly the one below his waist. It jutted impatiently against her.

He might as well have jabbed her with a hot poker, for the way she abruptly tore her mouth from his and stepped back. With a frustrated huff, she looked up and glared at him. "Good grief, Knox," she hissed. "You're supposed to be impotent. Could you at least try to stay in character?"

Knox blinked, astounded. In character? She'd been acting? Again?

Savannah looked down at the front of his tented *kurta*. Her lips curled into that oh-so-familiar mocking smile. "Well, at least the premature ejaculator part looks real. You've got a huge wet spot on the front of your dress."

Mortified, Knox felt a blush creep up his neck. "It's not a dress," he ground out.

Luckily the rest of the class had moved toward the refreshment table, which had been set up on the lawn. Only the Sheas lagged behind. To his further humiliation, the two of them noticed the evidence of his mortification and smiled knowingly.

"I see you've made progress already," Edgar said. "Embrace your healing, Knox," Edgar encouraged with a fatherly clap on the shoulder. "There's no shame in flaunting your seed. There is power in pro-creation.''

Rupali gestured toward Savannah's pearled nipples. ''Likewise, Barbie,'' she said mistily. ''You should be proud of your puckered breasts. They await your lover's kiss with tight invitation. Someday the milk of life will pour from those twin orbs. Flaunt them, as Edgar said.'' She smiled serenely, cupped her own breasts reverently. ''Embrace your femininity. Be proud of being a woman.''

Having blushed to the roots of her hair, Savannah managed a strained smile and nodded mutely. The Sheas threaded their fingers together and walked away, presumably to offer more little bits of tantric wisdom to other students.

Enjoying her discomfort, Knox smiled. ''I see I'm not the only one who had a hard time staying in character.''

Savannah closed her notebook and clipped her pen to the front. She gave him a blank look. ''I'm sorry, what?''

''Staying in character,'' he repeated. ''I'm not the only one who got hard.'' He stared pointedly at her breasts.

She gave him a frosty glare and her lips formed a withering smirk. ''I was cold, you moron. What's your excuse?''

His eyes narrowed. ''Your tongue was in my mouth.''

''And less of yours was in mine this time. Well

done, Knox. It's nice to know I'm not going to be choking on yours the entire weekend.''

No one could deliver a backhanded compliment quite like Savannah. Knox ignored the gibe and refused to let her change the subject. "You were not cold. You were hot, *damn hot,* and I could feel you.''

"How could you not feel me?" she asked, her voice climbing. "Edgar made us practically crawl into each other's *kurta*s. Basic physiological fact, Knox. The human body's normal temperature is ninety-eight-point-six degrees. That's hot and that's what you felt. End of story.''

The hell it was, Knox thought, but whatever. He didn't know what sort of insanity was eating at his brain to make him want to force her into admitting that something had happened between them. She was right to play it down. Keep it professional. He'd play it her way.

Or maybe not.

Knox shoved a hand through his hair and sighed heavily. "You're right. It is a little chilly out here today." Another lie. It was a pleasant seventy, at least.

Her gaze flew to his. "I'm right?" she asked, then nodded emphatically. "Right. Of course, I am.''

Knox suppressed a triumphant smile. So it was okay for her to lie about the attraction and make him feel like a class-A jackass, but apparently she didn't like wearing the shoe on the other foot.

Women, Knox thought. Had the Lord ever made a

more fickle creature? This was a prime example of why he'd never decided to keep one around on a permanent basis. They said yes when they meant no, and no when they meant yes. Who needed the grief? The confusion? Knox kept in touch with a select few women who knew him and knew the drill. Great date, great conversation, great sex. No strings. Everybody went home happy.

He would reluctantly admit that at times he longed for a deeper relationship, something more like his parents had. But so far he hadn't found anybody he'd want to spend a solid week with, much less the rest of his life. He was too preoccupied with the present to contemplate the future, at any rate.

Savannah could lie to him—and probably herself—all she wanted, but Knox knew the truth. Cold, hell. She'd been hot for him. If that kiss had been any hotter, the two of them would have surely gone up in flames. He'd never been so turned on from a mere kiss. Savannah Reeves had one talented mouth and it made Knox wonder just what other hidden abilities she possessed, and made him all the more determined to find out.

Without question, this unplanned, unwanted attraction posed many problems. For instance, how were they supposed to get through the rest of the weekend without going insane with lust? If he and Savannah detonated with heat over a couple of kisses, what would happen when they moved on to erotic massage, to *Love His Lingam*, and *Sacred*

Goddess Stimulation? What would happen on Sunday night, when the rest of the class was putting all their new know-how into practice? Furthermore, and more important, how on earth would he be able to maintain the focus needed to pull together an objective story if all he could think about was how much he wanted to plant himself between her thighs?

The two of them locked in various depraved positions flitted rapid fire through Knox's mind—his own personal little porn show where he and Savannah starred in hedonistic orgasmic splendor. He'd read the *Kama Sutra*. In his mind's eye Knox had her all but standing on her head when Savannah abruptly tapped him on the arm.

"Pay attention," she whispered. "They're about to resume the lecture."

Knox started, then moved to sit back down at their table. Savannah took her place beside him and, thankfully, began to take notes while Edgar and Rupali lectured on the importance of trust and announced that they would be doing a couple more little exercises before the lesson concluded for the day. They would have a great deal of "homework" this first night and would be provided ample time to get it all done.

In addition, all evening meals would be served in their rooms, with special instructions on how to enjoy them. Rupali and Edgar shared a secret smile that inspired equal parts curiosity and apprehension.

Great, Knox thought, as a wave of trepidation and anticipation washed over him. As if he didn't have enough to worry about.

SAVANNAH DIDN'T KNOW what was worse—attending the nerve-racking classes, or being alone with Knox. By the time they'd finished that last trust exercise, which she'd failed miserably at and which had consequently been added to their considerable homework, Savannah's raw nerves had been ready to snap. She'd tried to play off that second kiss with Knox, but it hadn't worked. Not by any stretch of the imagination.

He'd known, damn him.

She could see it in the cocky tilt of his head and the even cockier curve of his splendid lips. As if that gigantic ego of his needed another reason to swell, Savannah thought derisively. Even if he hadn't known then, he would have by the end of that lesson. Edgar and Rupali were firm believers in the oral chakra and the powers of kissing. According to Edgar and Rupali, the act taught patience to the men and promoted sexual harmony for the women. They'd had them necking at the end of each additional test, as well as the conclusion of the lecture. To her helpless joy and consternation, she and Knox had practically stayed in a perpetual lip-lock the rest of the afternoon.

If that hadn't been enough to shake her generally stalwart fortitude, there had been the *homework*.

When they'd returned to their room this afternoon,

they'd found several things awaiting them. Fresh *kurtas*, a new booklet that gave detailed information on how to unblock each of the chakras—and there was a lot more to it than even Savannah had realized—as well as instructions which had to be followed to the letter for the rest of the evening.

They were supposed to begin their evening with a shared bath.

Knox, damn him, had raised a hopeful eyebrow at this news, but Savannah had quickly disabused him of that notion.

The shared bath had also come with a few handy tips on how to enhance intimacy, like soaping your lover's body, washing each other's hair and light genital massage, along with the stern reminder that intercourse was forbidden.

Savannah had to admit that it sounded absolutely wonderful. That huge sunken marble tub might as well have had *Do It Here* written on little sticky notes scattered all over it—on the recessed steps, the back, the front and the side. It was a veritable Garden of Eden.

Furthermore, the idea of Knox's hands, slick with soap and hot water sliding all over her body was enough to send her heart rate into warp speed. Her palms actually tingled when she thought about giving him the same treatment, smoothing her own hands over the intriguing masculine landscape of his magnificent form. Over that incredible ass she'd finally gotten her greedy little hands on this afternoon. Honestly, she'd almost climaxed from the thrill of it.

She'd said no to the bath when she'd wanted to say yes, but to do anything different would have been a complete overthrow of her principles.

One of them had to remain focused and, though he'd claimed he'd brought her here because he didn't find her attractive, apparently Knox's primitive base instincts had overridden her general lack of appeal because, since that second kiss, he'd made absolutely no attempt to hold back.

In fact, Savannah grimly suspected he was goading her on purpose, arousing her for the pure sport of it. Because he knew he could, the bastard.

She had no idea how she should combat such an attack, but had finally decided that if he didn't back off soon, she'd launch an offensive of her own. If he continued to play with her and use her own reckless desire against her, Savannah would begin a similar assault upon his weakened libido and she'd have him begging for mercy.

While she'd lacked confidence in just about every other aspect of her life, there were two areas in which she knew she excelled. She was a damn fine journalist and, when she was with someone she trusted without question, a sadly rare occurrence, she was one hell of a lover.

Savannah might not have had as many partners as Knox, but it wasn't so much the quantity as the quality, and she'd never failed to satisfy a man in the bedroom. Savannah enjoyed sex, was very uninhibited, and those qualities came through in her performance. In fact, she'd never had bad sex. If her partner didn't do it for her, she'd simply roll him over and take care of matters herself. Savannah grinned. What man didn't like that?

There was something so elemental, so raw and intense when it came to sex. Any pent-up emotion could be vented, exorcised, and the simple act made her feel more human, more connected, than any other.

And it had been too long, Savannah thought with a despondent sigh. She imagined the combined factors of sexual deprivation and Knox were the reason she was so rabidly horny now. She hadn't made love since Gib.

Initially she'd been too hurt to even consider building a relationship with another man. Then once she'd gotten past that point, her career had begun to take off and there simply hadn't been time.

Savannah didn't do casual sex. In addition to it not being safe, there was nothing casual about sharing your body with another person. At least, not for her. Her character had not been formed for that increasingly popular pastime and she'd just as soon go without.

Until now.

Now she'd become the proverbial bitch in heat. She wanted Knox—had always wanted Knox—but had managed to keep the attraction under control by avoiding him as much as possible and by generally striving to be the most unpleasant person on the face of the planet anytime he was around.

But she couldn't do that now. They were here, sharing a room, and while he might sound like Gib, and occasionally act like Gib, Savannah knew her desire to dislike Knox had been more of a defense mechanism than anything else. Just a way to prevent herself from liking him because she didn't want to make the same mistake twice.

Knox chose that particular moment to open the bathroom door. Scented steam billowed from behind him as he strolled in all his almost-naked glory to the bed to retrieve his clean *kurta*. He'd anchored a bath sheet loosely about his waist and a few small droplets of water skidded down the bumpy planes of his ridged abdomen. An inverted triangle of dark brown hair dusted his chest and arrowed into a slim line that bisected that washboard abdomen and disappeared beneath the line of his towel.

His muscular legs and arms were covered in the same smattering of hair, and had it continued around to his back like a pelt, Savannah might have stood a prayer of not melting into a puddle of panting female at the mere sight of his practically naked body.

But it didn't.

He was perfect, damn him, and she hungered for him as if she hadn't eaten in weeks and he were a decadent slab of prime rib.

She swallowed and did her best to rid her expression of any lingering lust. "You've been in there forever. I-is there any hot water left?" She strove for a put-out tone, but the sound was more breathless than irritated.

"Yeah," he said distractedly. His brow puckered and he lifted the *kurta* from the bed, tossed it aside and glanced at the floor. He bent over and checked beneath the bed skirt, and then paused, seemingly at a loss. He settled his hands at his hips, causing every well-formed muscle to ripple invitingly. Particularly his pecs. Savannah had always been a sucker for a gorgeous set of pecs.

"Have you lost something?" Savannah asked.

"Yeah. My underwear. Have you seen them?"

He knew perfectly well that they weren't allowed to wear any underwear. He was simply trying to annoy her, to remind her that he wouldn't be wearing any. Savannah glanced to the prominent bulge beneath his towel and sighed. As if she'd need reminding.

"No, sorry. I haven't." She smiled sweetly. "I seem to have lost mine as well. While you're looking for yours, why don't you be a dear and look for mine, too?"

Surprised, his patently perplexed expression vanished and he slowly looked up. A playful gleam suddenly lit his gaze. "Sure. I'd be happy to. Er...wanna tell me what they look like?"

Uh-oh. This wasn't exactly the scenario she'd hoped for. For some reason, she'd thought he'd feign sudden inspiration and laughingly remember the no-undergarment rule. She should have known better. He rarely resisted a challenge.

Still Knox needed to know whom he was dealing with, and this seemed to be as good a way as any to teach him, Savannah decided, warming to her tact.

"They're black silk. There's not much to them, barely a scrap of fabric. You might have a hard time finding them."

Knox's eyes darkened and she watched the muscles in his throat work as he swallowed. Feeling decidedly triumphant, Savannah stood and started toward the bathroom.

"Black silk, eh?" Knox said, his voice somewhat rusty. "Are there, uh, any distinguishing features? Anything that would make them more recognizable?"

Savannah paused with her hand on the doorknob and turned around. Her amused you're-playing-with-fire gaze met his and held it. "Yeah. They're thong underwear. Black lace with little black pearls."

Silence thundered between them at this glib description, then, his eyes never leaving hers, Knox casually dropped his towel. The sheer power—utter perfection and beauty—of his nude body rooted Savannah to the floor.

Seeing an outline of his penis hadn't prepared her for the actual article. He was only semiaroused, yet huge and proud—as he most certainly had every right to be—and every cell in her body responded to the blatantly virile part of him. She couldn't have looked away if she'd wanted to.

Knox picked up the *kurta* and, with a sexy grin, said, "Pity we can't wear underwear this weekend. I'd love to get a peek at that particular pair of panties. If you find them, why don't you show them to me?" He paused and his voice lowered to a more intimate level, sending a chorus of shivers down her spine. "I'll bet you look great in them."

Savannah determinedly ignored her initial impulse, which was to walk across the room, drop to her knees and suck him dry. Another talent of hers, if she did say so herself.

However, she would not let him win this little scene.

She'd been prepared for a battle royal and the smug devil thought he'd gotten the better of her with this little display. He'd best think again. She'd seen a dick before. Granted not one as splendidly formed as his, but she was familiar enough with the male anatomy not to look like the shocked little virgin he apparently expected.

Savannah shot him a confident grin. "Not nearly as good as I look *out* of them."

With an exaggerated swing of her hips, she sauntered into the bathroom and shut the door.

Then she ran her bath, settled into the hot fragrant water, and imagined a naked Knox on the other side of the door…imagined everything she'd ever wanted to do with him and to him and everything she'd ever wanted him to do to her....

With a frustrated groan of the hopelessly, futilely aroused, she spread her thighs, parted her curls and, with a whimper of satisfaction...pulled a Chuck.

7

_____

SAVANNAH APPEARED considerably less tense after her bath, Knox noted. Her movements were languid, leisurely and there was something altogether relaxed about her. She'd towel-dried her hair and the blue-black locks curled madly around her face, sprouting up in chaotic disarray all over her head like little question marks. She looked charmingly unkempt as always. He grinned. Even wet, she looked messy. She'd removed her makeup and her pale skin glowed with health and vitality. Her cheeks held a rosy hue and that plump bottom lip looked a little swollen, as though she'd been chewing on it.

Knox felt his eyes narrow and suspiciously considered her once more.

Relaxed, rosy and a swollen bottom lip. She'd obviously had more than a bath, Knox realized, astonished. He knew perfectly well what a woman looked like after release and clearly, by the sated look of her, she'd had a damn good one. He didn't know whether to be irritated or pleased. Irritated because he would have gladly taken care of her—would have loved to have brought her to climax—or pleased because she'd been so hot for him she'd had to take care of herself.

He decided to be pleased and covertly considered her once more. It was a rare woman who felt comfortable enough with her body to tend to her own needs. In his experience, women loved to be touched but didn't necessarily enjoy touching themselves. Clearly Savannah didn't suffer from any such inhibition. A snake of heat writhed through his belly at the thought. But that's the kind of woman she was. She would never rely solely on a man to get what she wanted, Knox thought with reluctant admiration. She had to be the most self-reliant woman he'd ever known.

Once again Knox wondered about her past. Just who exactly was Savannah Reeves? What had made her so independent, so determined to be an island unto herself? What had made her into this distrustful, autonomic loner? He knew absolutely nothing about her, he realized. Where she'd grown up, whether or not she had any brothers and sisters—nothing.

What was *her* story? he wondered, and felt a familiar nudge. Knox didn't know, but he firmly intended to find out before this weekend was up. Right now, however, they had other issues to deal with.

Like dinner.

A wonderful spread complete with all the romantic trimmings had arrived just moments before she'd walked out of the bathroom and distracted him. Knox had had a moment to peruse the instructions and he strongly suspected that Savannah would not enjoy their next assignment.

Which meant he wouldn't either because he would starve.

"Did you enjoy your bath?" Knox asked lightly.

Savannah pilfered through her toiletries until she located a bottle of moisturizer, uncapped the lid and poured a little into the palm of her hand, then began to massage the cream onto her face and neck. "Immensely," she all but sighed. "That's a great tub."

"Yeah, it is," he agreed, imagining her naked in it, her little fingers nestled in her curls and her head thrown back in orgasmic wonder.

Savannah's gaze lit upon the dining cart and a smile bloomed on her slightly swollen lips. "Oh, good. The food's here. I'm *starving.*"

Knox smiled knowingly. He'd just bet she was. Having a bone-melting climax typically did that to a person. Still, he had a feeling she was about to lose her appetite.

Savannah made her way across the room and inspected their meal. She took a deep breath, savoring the hickory scent of grilled steak tips with sautéed mushrooms, au gratin potatoes and steamed asparagus. "Oh, this looks heavenly," she groaned with pleasure.

Wondering how long it would take her to figure out what was wrong with the *heavenly* meal, Knox started to count. *One…*

She moved things around on the tray. "I love steak. And this looks wonderful."

Two...

"And I haven't had it in a long time. What a treat." Her brow wrinkled. "Hey, where's the—"

Three.

"—silverware?"

"There isn't any."

Her head jerked up and her delighted expression vanished. "What?"

"There isn't any," Knox repeated. He rattled the instructions for their meal in his hand meaningfully. "Here're our instructions. Would you like to read them yourself or would you rather I summarize them for you?"

Predictably, Savannah marched across and the room and snatched the sheet from his hand. "I'll read them myself, thank you."

Three beats passed before she'd gotten past the mystical mumbo jumbo and found out why they didn't have any utensils. Her outraged gasp sounded, and then she glared at Knox as though it were *his* fault. As though this were his idea. Hell, he hadn't made the rules.

"Feed each other?" she growled with a lethally icy look. "It's not enough that you've hauled me across the country to this godforsaken workshop, that I've had your tongue down my throat all blessed day, and now—*now*—if I want to have anything to eat it has to come from your fingers?" she asked incredulously. Those chilly blue eyes blasted him with another arctic look. She crossed her arms over her chest and, with a grim disbelieving look, she shook her head. "This is insane and is *so* not going to happen."

Knox shrugged. "I thought it sounded fun."

She snorted. "You would."

"And I'm hungry."

She hugged her arms closer around her middle and gazed longingly at the tray. "I was."

Knox paused, then said, "I agree that the shared bath was an unreasonable expectation, one I would have done had you been willing. But surely we could at least make an effort with this exercise." He lifted a shoulder. "Like you said, we've been kissing all day. How could me feeding you be any more personal? We've got to participate in as many of these exercises as we comfortably can to lend credibility to our story, to do our best work. What's the big deal?"

Indecision flashed in her eyes. She fidgeted and glanced back at the dining cart with another woebegone look. He knew he had her when her stomach rumbled. Knox suppressed a triumphant grin.

"Oh, all right," she finally relented. "But no funny stuff, Knox. I'm hungry. I want to eat, unblock a few chakras and go to bed."

Savannah pivoted, stalked back to the dining cart and swiftly began to move the plates and glasses onto the table. She didn't bother with the fresh-cut flowers and bent over and extinguished the candle with a determined breath.

Knox waited until she'd finished arranging things to her satisfaction and then joined her at the table. "What would you like to start with?"

"Oh, no," she said with a calculating grin. "I'll feed you a bite first, that way you'll understand exactly how I want you to feed me."

Knox knew he was going to enjoy this too much not to be at least a little accommodating. He nodded. "Fine."

Her cheeks puffed as she exhaled mightily. "So, what do you want to start with?"

"Steak."

Savannah picked up a steak tip. "Okay. Open up."

Knox did. Her fingers stopped just shy of his lips and she tossed it into his mouth so hard it bounced off the back of his throat and almost back out of his mouth. Knox managed to hang on to it and, smiling at her ingenuity, chewed the tasty morsel. This was not going as he'd planned. Next she'd be catapulting potatoes into his mouth and throwing asparagus at him like javelins.

And she looked so damned pleased with herself, Knox thought. Those clear blue orbs sparkled with unrepentant laughter.

Knox finally swallowed, cleared his throat and gave her a droll look. "I'll need to see you balance a ball on your nose before I feed you like a seal."

Tongue in cheek, her lips twitched. "I didn't mean to throw it quite s-so hard."

"Right." It was his turn. He selected a steak tip and held it up for her inspection. "Ready?"

She nodded and hesitantly opened her mouth. Knox fed her the bite without incident and was careful not to let his fingers linger. He wanted her at ease, not guarded. This, too, was another trust builder and Savannah so desperately needed to learn to trust someone.

Knox had decided that person should be him.

He didn't know when he'd come to the decision or, for that matter, even why. But he wanted to be worthy of her trust. Wanted to be the person who brought her out of her isolated existence. He supposed he'd fully realized the extent of her distrustful nature this afternoon when they'd been practicing another faith-building exercise. It should have been simple. All Savannah had to do was stand in front of him, fall backward and allow Knox to catch her.

She couldn't do it.

Just as she'd start to fall backward, she'd abruptly stop and right herself. They practiced over and over again. But for all that work, she still hadn't been able to trust him enough to catch her. As a result, they were supposed to practice that exercise tonight, too. An idea occurred to him.

"Why don't we look at that chakra homework while we're eating dinner?" he asked.

Savannah nodded. "That's a good idea. Don't touch anything. I'll get the book."

She double-timed it back and opened the volume to the appropriate page. "Give me another bite of steak, would you?" she said as she perused the page.

She absently opened her mouth for three more bites before Knox finally laughed and said, "Hey, what about me?"

Distracted, Savannah picked up a bite of steak and placed it on his tongue, then unwittingly licked her fingers.

His dick jerked beneath the *kurta*.

"Okay," she said. "We'll pass this book back and forth. I'll start with the first one, which is the perineum chakra or root chakra," she said. "Then you can take—"

"Er…why don't we skip that one?" Knox suggested. He knew all he needed to know about that particular chakra.

"Consider the story, tight-ass," she said with an infuriating little grin. "We'd hate to mislead our readers by not having all the facts."

"I'm not a tight-ass," Knox growled.

She grinned. "Hit a nerve, did I?"

"I'm driven. That doesn't make me a tight-ass—it makes me a professional."

She tsked under her breath. "A professional wouldn't balk at learning about his root chakra… unless he was a tight-ass."

Knox heaved a mighty sigh. "Fine. Gimme some potatoes, would you?"

Savannah tensed but loaded the requested side dish onto a couple of fingers and gave him a bite. Knox wrapped his lips around her fingers, sucked the potatoes off and sighed with satisfaction. "Mmm," he groaned. "Those are good. Want some?" he asked innocently.

Her shoulders rounded and she shot him a put-upon look. "Oh, hell. Why not? Yes," she sighed. "I do."

Knox curved a couple of fingers and scooped up a generous bite and ladled it into her mouth. Her eyes rounded with delighted wonder. "Oh," she said thickly. And then, "Ohh, these are great. More, more."

Laughing, Knox scooped up another helping and she wasn't so quick to avoid his fingers this time. She actually licked off a hunk of cheese that she'd missed on the first go around from his index finger. The slide of that tongue felt great and it didn't take much imagination to picture her lips wrapped around another prominent part of his anatomy. Still, she'd just begun to marginally relax, so Knox tried to appear unaffected.

He nodded to his plate. "How about letting me try that asparagus?"

"Sure." She picked up a spear and fed it to him. "What do you think? Is it good, or should we stick with the steak and potatoes?"

Swallowing, Knox nodded. "It's good, too. Hell, all of it's good." He inspected the table. "What did we get for dessert?"

Savannah peeked beneath a couple of smaller lids and her eyes all but rolled back in her head. A purr of delight emanated from her throat. "Strawberries and fresh cream. Forget the chakras. Let's eat. We can study later."

"Agreed."

Without further discussion, they promptly began to feed each other. Savannah loaded her fingers while sucking her bites from his and vice versa. Knox made sure that he got a suggestive lick in every third or fourth bite, but rather than giving him a frosty glare, Savannah eventually began to take it as a challenge. Sucking particularly hard one time, giving a clever flick of her facile tongue another. She was so damned competitive, she didn't intend for him ever to get the upper hand. Big surprise there, Knox thought. She took everything as a challenge and he seemed to be her favorite opponent.

Knox tolerated the main course with amazing restraint, but began to have a problem when they moved on to dessert. Watching Savannah's lips pucker around a strawberry, watching her lick the cream from his finger and around her mouth without having a screaming orgasm was proving to be damned difficult. To be honest, he didn't particularly like strawberries, but kept eating them anyway so that he could taste her fingers. He'd never imagined that feeding someone, or being fed, could be so damned erotic.

But it was.

And they'd get to repeat the whole process tomorrow night, and the next.

Savannah polished off the last strawberry with a deep sigh of satisfaction. Her tongue made a slow lap around her lips, making sure that she'd savored every bit of the arousing dessert. "That," she said meaningfully, "was excellent."

Without a doubt, Knox thought. He seriously doubted he'd ever eat again without thinking about this experience. Gave a whole new meaning to the term finger foods.

Savannah stood, placed her palms on the small of her back and stretched. *Newton's Third Law: For every action there is an equal and opposite reaction.* For reasons that escaped him, this was the thought that tripped through his head as Savannah's naked breasts were pushed up and against the thin fabric of her gown. He longed to taste her through the fabric, to draw the crown of that creamy breast into his mouth.

Savannah finally relaxed. "I'll wheel this dining cart out into the hall, then we'll get started on our chakra lessons."

"Fine." Knox lay down at the foot of the bed.

Her step faltered on her return trip to the table. "What are you doing?"

He gestured to the bedside lamps. "Better lighting."

"Right." She smirked.

Oh, hell. One step forward, two steps back. She didn't drop her guard for anything. "You can lean against the headboard," Knox told her. "We'll be more comfortable."

"There is that. You'll need to be comfortable when we unblock your perineum chakra."

"My perineum chakra isn't blocked," Knox said through gritted teeth.

"We'll see," she said maddeningly.

Savannah retrieved the book, then did as Knox suggested and settled herself against the headboard of the bed. The bedside light cast part of her face in shadow and the other in stark relief. The pure white gown practically glowed, giving her an almost ethereal appearance. Knox swallowed as an unfamiliar emotion clogged his throat. If he'd ever seen a more beautiful woman, he couldn't recall.

"Okay," she sighed. "Let's get down to business." She read for a moment and then her laughing gaze tangled with his. "According to this, the root chakra deals with the desire to own and possess. People who have difficulty expressing themselves, who limit spontaneity, and are inflexible are generally tense in this chakra." She gave him a pointed look. "In short, they are tight-asses. Like you." She frowned innocently. "Do you have a problem with hemorrhoids, Knox?"

His lips twisted into a sardonic smile. "Right now, you're the only pain in my ass."

She laughed—actually laughed out load, a femininely melodious sound. He'd worked with her for over a year and had never heard her more than chuckle briefly. Another breakthrough, Knox decided, irrationally pleased with himself.

"In order to unblock this chakra, you're supposed to insert your finger into your lover's *rosebud* and—"

Knox felt his butt draw up again. "*What?* What's a rosebud?"

She grinned evilly. "It's tantric slang for asshole."

"Nobody is going to insert anything into my rosebud," Knox said flatly.

"It won't bloom," Savannah warned.

"Good."

Wearing a wicked smile, she shrugged. "Okay, for the sake of our respective rosebuds, let's just assume that neither one of us is blocked in the root chakra."

Knox felt his ass relax. "That'll work for me."

Savannah read on for a moment, then looked up. "Okay, we're supposed to align our chakras, express our love—"

Knox sat up. "Align? Did you say align?"

"Yes."

He smiled triumphantly. "And isn't that what I told you we were supposed to do in the first place?"

Savannah gazed at him. "You might have," she admitted hesitantly.

He collapsed onto the bed once more. "I knew it. I knew we were supposed to align something, by God."

She heaved an exasperated sigh. "You don't align your chakras until you unblock them. We've unblocked our root chakra. Now we align, express our love, and chant *lam.*"

Savannah set the book aside, moved away from the headboard and lay down in front of Knox. "We're aligned. Now chant."

Knox frowned. "You call this aligned? Shouldn't you be closer?" He gestured to the thirty-six inches that yawned between them.

"This'll do."

Knox shook his head doubtfully, snaked an arm around her waist and tugged her toward him. He fitted her snugly up next to his body and growled low in his throat. "Now *this* is aligned."

She looked up at him and twin devils danced in her eyes. She batted her lashes. "Express your love, Knox."

Knox grinned. "I love your ass."

Another laugh bubbled up, making her shake against him. She smelled like strawberries and cream and apple lotion, and she felt utterly incredible in his arms. Lust licked at his veins, stirred in his loins.

"That'll do," she finally replied. "Let's chant. *Laaaammmmmm. Laaaammmmmm.*"

Knox made a halfhearted attempt but couldn't continue. The absolute absurdity of it hit him and he'd begun to laugh and couldn't stop. "Can you believe that right now, while we're lying here, people in this house are having their r-rosebuds digitally probed and are chanting this stuff?"

Savannah giggled. "And Chuck's probably whacking off."

Knox guffawed until his sides hurt, then rolled over onto his back and smoothed his hair off his forehead. He blew out a breath. "Because they think that this is going to cure them, that this tantric stuff is going to fix whatever is wrong with their lives."

Savannah's chuckled tittered out. "It's kind of sad, huh?"

"Yeah," Knox admitted solemnly. "It really is."

"If it doesn't work, we'll report it," she said at last. "That's what we do."

"I know."

"I'm looking forward to writing this story," she admitted, much to his surprise.

"*We're* writing," Knox felt compelled to point out. "*We're* writing this story."

"About that…" She winced. "Just exactly how are we supposed to do this story? I've always worked alone—I've never collaborated on an article before."

"Neither have I," Knox confessed. "I suppose we should just toss out ideas until the right one fits and go from there."

"What if we don't agree? What if you don't like my ideas and I don't like yours? Then what?"

He shot her a look. "Sounds like you've already made up your mind to hate my ideas."

She grinned. "Well, of course."

Another laugh rumbled from his chest. "Don't hold back, Savannah. Tell me how you really feel." Knox sighed. "I don't know. Let's just cross that bridge when we come to it. We're still a long way from putting pen to paper."

Savannah's breath left her in a small whoosh and she pulled away from him and sat up. "I don't know about you, but I'm tired and don't feel like having anything else unblocked and aligned tonight."

"Nah, me neither."

Knox sat up as well. He snagged a pillow from the bed and found a spare blanket in the chest of drawers. Sleeping on the floor didn't appeal to him whatsoever, but he'd made a great deal of progress with Savannah tonight and he didn't want to jeopardize it by begging for a spot in the bed. He fixed his pallet on top of the floor pillows and gingerly lowered himself onto the lumpy makeshift bed.

"G'night, Knox," Savannah murmured.

He smiled and glanced up at her. "Night." *See, he mentally telegraphed to her, see how damned sweet I can be?* She turned off the light, plunging the room into darkness.

He heard Savannah settle in and sigh with satisfaction. Knox twisted and turned, fluffed and flattened pillows. Hell, he'd be better off sleeping in the damned bathtub, he decided, after several failed attempts to get comfortable. He groaned miserably and rolled over again, this time cracking his elbow painfully against the wall.

Savannah heaved a beleaguered breath. "Oh, for pity's sake, Knox, just get in the bed."

He stilled. "Really?"

"Yes," she huffed. "I suppose if I can kiss you all day and eat from your fingers, I can stand to have you sleep beside me. Just stay on your side and keep your hands to yourself."

Knox happily hoisted himself from the lumpy pillows, trotted over to the bed and slid under the covers. He thought he heard Savannah whimper when his weight shifted the mattress.

"Are you all right?" he asked.

He felt her move onto her back. "I'm fine." She paused. "Look, Knox, I'm used to sleeping alone, so I generally hog the whole bed. If I roll onto you, or crowd you, just shove me back onto my own side."

"Sure," he said, mildly perplexed. Was she a thrasher or something? he wondered. "I'm used to sleeping alone, too. You do the same for me."

"I will." Something ominous lurked in her tone.

Knox smiled. "G'night, Vannah."

She rolled onto her side once more, giving him her back. "It's *Savannah*," she growled. "Now shut up so that I can get come sleep."

There's my girl, Knox thought with a sleepy smile. His bitch was back. Funny, but she didn't sound so tough anymore. Knox heard the fear and vulnerability behind the surly attitude. What would it take, he wondered, to make her lose that edge? To strip away the destructive defenses and build her back up with a more productive emotion?

Knox didn't know, but he was grimly determined to find out.

8

SAVANNAH AWOKE early in the exact position she'd feared she would—draped all over Knox.

Presently her cheek lay cuddled up to his sinewy shoulder, her arm was anchored around his lean waist and she'd slung a thigh over his delectable rear. Jeez, even in her sleep she couldn't resist him. Savannah knew that she should carefully extricate herself from him before he woke up and found her melted all over him, but she couldn't summon the necessary actions to move away just yet.

He felt…nice.

His big, warm body threw off a heat like a blast furnace, chasing away the early morning chill. She breathed in a hint of woodsy aftershave and male, and the particular essence that was simply Knox, and felt a twine of heat curl though her belly, lick her nipples and settle in her sex.

Savannah was accustomed to waking up hungry, but the appetite that plagued her this morning wouldn't be satisfied with a mere muffin and a cup of coffee. She wanted an order of Knox with hot, sweaty sex on the side.

On the side of the bed.

On the side of the tub.

Her side.

His side.

Inside or outside.

Any side.

She honestly didn't care. Savannah bit back a groan of frustration. She was starving here, starving for him and the hunger had all but gotten the best of her.

Savannah had set out on this confounded assignment against her will, wholly determined to resist Knox. She'd known that the story had immense potential, and she hadn't underestimated her attraction, but she had underestimated Knox.

He wasn't the shallow, thoughtless, lazy playboy she'd forced herself to believe he was.

Some innate sense of self-preservation had kicked in when she'd first met him, because her subconscious had recognized him as a potential threat to her heart. Savannah had looked at him and unfairly projected each and every one of Gib's character flaws upon Knox.

While the character flaws had been false, one glaring fact still remained—Knox still posed a threat to her heart. If she let down her guard one whit, Savannah knew Knox would burrow beneath her defenses, fasten himself onto that traitorous organ and, short of a transplant, she'd never get rid of him.

He wouldn't have a problem getting rid of her,

though, Savannah thought with a bitter smile. No one ever did. That's why, regardless of how charming and witty, how adorable and sweet—how sexy—he turned out to be, she had to keep things in perspective. Keep her defenses in place.

They'd spent scarcely twenty-four hours together and, nerve-racking kisses and chronic masturbators aside, Savannah had had more fun in this single day with Knox than she'd had in years. He'd made her laugh, a rare feat. Sad, Savannah realized, but true. Given the opportunity, she wondered, what other rare feats could Knox facilitate? What other hidden talents did he have?

He stirred beside her and Savannah tensed and held her breath, silently praying that he wouldn't wake up and find her all but planting a flag in his groin. He didn't. But to Savannah's immense pleasure and frustration, he wrapped his hand around hers and, murmuring nonsensical sounds, tugged her even closer than she'd been before. Her breasts were now completely flattened against his muscular back and, of course, reacted accordingly. They grew heavy with want and her nipples hardened into tight, sensitive peaks. Her clit throbbed a steady mantra of *I'm ready!* One clever touch, Savannah knew, and she'd shatter.

Knox, damn him, was asleep, completely oblivious to her torture and exempt from his own.

Well, Savannah thought, she could either lie there and simmer in her sexually frustrated misery, or she could get up and try to put a more productive spin on the morning. Breakfast would be served in the common room at eight, and another lecture—more erotic massage—would begin promptly at nine. This lecture in particular was supposed to be one of those graphic, hands-on demonstrations the Sheas' brochures had promised and would segue into tomorrow's *Love His Lingam* and *Sacred Goddess Stimulation.* Savannah both dreaded and looked forward to those lessons. She'd be less than honest if she didn't admit to at least some morbid fascination.

Besides, she liked to excel at everything and if she gleaned even the slightest knowledge on how to please a future lover—or please herself—then she'd leave this damned workshop better than she arrived.

A careful look at the bedside clock told her that she and Knox needed to get the lead out. They'd only unblocked one chakra and had totally skipped her building-trust homework. Humiliation burned Savannah's cheeks. Naturally she knew that she had certain trust issues—she'd never been in a relationship in her life that hadn't ended in some form of disappointment. But she hadn't realized the true extent of her distrust until yesterday. She'd been the only person in the entire class who'd flunked the "blind trust" test. The symbolism hadn't been lost on her or, more embarrassingly, him.

All she'd had to do was stand with her back to Knox, fall backward and let him catch her. Most couples had nailed it on the first try. She and Knox had attempted the exercise until the end of class and she still hadn't gotten it. Edgar and Rupali had shared an enigmatic look, then instructed her and Knox to work on the exercise for homework.

Quite frankly, Savannah didn't give a rip what the Sheas or any of these other people here thought about her. Beyond this weekend she'd never see them again. But that wasn't the case with Knox. She'd see him on a day-to-day basis and, during that idiotic test, she'd had the uneasy privilege of watching his emotions leap from teasing mockery to pity and, finally, to curiosity.

It wouldn't be enough that he knew she had trust issues—he was a journalist and would have to know *why.* If she wouldn't tell him when he covertly interviewed her—and she had no doubt whatsoever that he would—he'd dig around until he raked up every bit of her unfortunate past. She inwardly shuddered with dread.

She'd become a *story,* Savannah realized, an exposé, and Knox, despite his laid-back attitude, was nothing short of a bloodhound when he caught the scent of a story. He'd use his particular brand of talent to unearth every unpleasant aspect of her past and he'd pull one of his legendary show-and-tell tactics on her. While she'd love to play a little show-and-tell with him, she didn't want it to have anything to do with her private life.

Despite her present predicament with Chapman, Savannah had a good reputation at the *Phoenix.*

She'd worked hard to garner the respect of her peers, and if Knox used his trademark talent on her, she'd have to watch that respect become tempered with pity.

She would not be anyone's object of pity.

Savannah was wondering what tack she should take when Knox abruptly stirred once more. He stretched beside her, yawned, and she knew the exact instant when he awakened and the full realization of their position registered, because he grew completely still. Then he abruptly relaxed and she didn't have to see his face to know that he undoubtedly wore a cat-in-the-cream expression.

Feigning sleep, Savannah moaned softly and nonchalantly rolled away from him and onto her side. There, she thought. She'd escaped. She'd saved face and would—

To Savannah's slack-jawed astonishment, using the exact same tactic she'd just employed, Knox promptly spooned her. The force of his heat engulfed her as he bellied up to her back. He twined an arm around her middle and unerringly settled his palm upon her breast. Savannah hadn't recovered from that brazen move before he pushed his thigh between her legs and sighed with audible satisfaction right into her ear. The combined masculine weight, heat and scent of him caused a tornado of sensation to erupt below her navel.

She couldn't believe his gall. At least she'd molested him while she'd been asleep and unaware of her transgressions. Knox, the sneaky lout, was in full possession of his senses and had used the lucky opportunity to take advantage of the situation. Still, her conscience needled, she hadn't abruptly drawn away from him when she'd woken up. She'd lain there and savored the feel of him against her, just as she was doing now.

Which was madness, she thought with a spurt of self-loathing. Why didn't she just forgo all of the niceties and hand him her heart to break?

Savannah drove her elbow into his unsuspecting stomach. "Get...off...me."

Knox's breath left him in a quick, surprised whoosh and he promptly released her throbbing breast and rolled away. "Wh-what?" he asked with enough sleepy perplexity to look genuine. But she knew better.

Savannah glared at him. "I thought I told you to stay on your side of the bed."

Knox sat up in bed and rubbed a hand over the back of his neck. His mink-brown hair was mussed and the flush of sleep still clung to his cheeks. Those heavy-lidded eyes were weighted even more with the dregs of slumber. He looked almost boyish, yet the term didn't quite fit, because there was absolutely nothing boyish about the way her body reacted to his.

"Huh?" he managed.

Savannah blew out a breath. "I thought I told you to stay on your side of the bed," she repeated.

"Didn't I?" he asked foggily.

He knew damn well he hadn't, the wretch. "No," she said tightly. "You did not."

He frowned. "Oh, sorry. Hope I didn't crowd you."

"I woke up with your hand wrapped around my breast."

A smile quivered on his lips. Knox threw the covers off and planted his feet on the floor, but didn't readily stand. He leveled a droll look at her. "Funny. I woke up with your hand inches above my dick and your thigh on my ass, but you don't hear me complaining."

Savannah flushed. She could win this argument, but not without admitting fault on her own part, so she didn't bother. "Just get ready," she huffed. "We've got less than an hour before breakfast."

THEY WERE TEN MINUTES LATE for breakfast. Knox had been wrong. Savannah did take great pains with her hair—it just didn't do any good.

She'd spent the better part of thirty minutes this morning trying to force the unruly locks into some semblance of a true style and when she'd finally exited the bathroom, she'd looked exactly as she had when she'd gone in. "I don't know why I bother," she said when she walked out.

Knox had bitten his tongue to keep from saying, "Me, neither."

He kept his mouth shut, of course. He'd already

pissed her off this morning with the sleepy-hand-upon-her-breast bit and didn't dare risk her further displeasure by agreeing with her dead-on assessment about her hair. Besides, her hair had character. Knox thought it was adorable.

Having her draped all over him this morning had been a pleasant surprise. She'd smelled curiously like apples, a scent he'd associated with her before, and the feminine weight of her body nuzzled against his had been incredible. He'd felt the press of those delectable nipples against his back and that sweet hand snugged against his abdomen. If she hadn't moved when she did, his randy pecker would have nudged under her palm like an eager puppy begging for a stroke.

He'd known he shouldn't have rolled over with her, but for some perverse reason, he hadn't been able to help himself. His palms literally itched to touch her.

The one woman he'd imagined he wouldn't be hot for had unaccountably turned into the one woman he simply had to have.

Knox had never in his life longed to root himself between a woman's thighs more. He wanted her legs hooked over his shoulders, her arms lashed around his waist and her tongue in his mouth, and not necessarily in that order.

A moment after they entered, the Sheas moved to stand side by side in front of the room and garnered everyone's attention. "Greetings and good morning to you,'' Rupali said. Knox noticed that when Rupali moved forward to speak, Edgar instinctively moved slightly back and behind her. Support, Knox realized with a jolt of surprise and admiration. ''We hope that you all passed a pleasant night and adhered to the rules set out for this retreat.'' She paused. ''Did everyone adhere to the rules?''

A chorus of assents passed through the room, though Knox spotted at least two guilty faces. One was Chuck's, of course.

''What about homework?'' Edgar asked. This time, it was Rupali that moved behind him. So the respect and support was reciprocated, not just one-sided.

Despite all of the questions and doubts surrounding this workshop and tantric sex in general, Knox had to admit that their relationship seemed genuine. They obviously cared very deeply for each other.

What would it be like to be on the receiving end of such unwavering love and support? Knox wondered as a curious void suddenly shifted in his chest. What would it be like to have someone who believed in you so much that they instinctively knew to get behind you when you needed it, or perhaps even when you didn't? He'd had that sort of support from his family until he'd majored in journalism, but after that he'd lost their encouragement. It had hurt, but the desire to succeed had been a balm to his disappointment.

''Let's have a status report on our chakras,'' Edgar

said. "We'll start and go around the room. Tell what sort of breakthroughs you experienced, as well as how many chakras you believe you unblocked. Who would like to go first?"

Several hands shot into the air at this question. Needless to say, his and Savannah's weren't among them. Chuck and Marge began and proudly reported that they'd unblocked their perineum, genital and belly chakras. Several other couples continued in this vein sharing their experiences, reporting multiple chakra breakthroughs. Knox began to get a little nervous. He hadn't realized just how little he and Savannah had gotten done last night. They'd have to take their break this afternoon and play some catch-up; otherwise they were going to be lagging behind the rest of the class. That was simply unacceptable. Knox didn't lag behind anyone.

Apparently, the realization had hit Savannah as well. Her lips had flattened into an adorably mulish expression. Knox felt his lips twitch. He knew that look—heaven knows he'd seen it often enough—and it meant watch your back.

"Is there anyone who hasn't reported?" Rupali asked.

"Knox and Barbie haven't," Marge replied helpfully. Knox gritted his teeth and smiled at her.

"Well, Knox and Barbie," Rupali said. "How did it go?"

Knox looked to Savannah, hoping in her ire, she'd step up and answer the question. For all appearances she smiled encouragingly, but Knox saw the evil humor dancing in that ice-blue gaze. Her look clearly said, "You made your bed, now lie in it."

"We, uh, worked on the trust exercise so much that we only got the r-root chakra unblocked," Knox reported. From the corner of his eye, he saw Savannah's eyes narrow fractionally. Obviously, she didn't appreciate taking the blame for their poor performance.

"Don't be so modest, baby," Savannah said sweetly. "Tell the rest."

The rest? Knox wondered as his breakfast curdled in his stomach. His smile froze. "That's private, pumpkin," he all but growled through gritted teeth. He had absolutely no idea what she was talking about, but instinctively knew she intended to humiliate him. Royally.

"Nothing is private here, Knox," Rupali reminded with a smile. "Truth and healing, remember? You obviously have something to be proud of. Barbie is proud. Please share," she encouraged gently.

"I—"

"Oh, very well," Savannah said, with a humbly mysterious look about the room. "I'll tell them." She paused dramatically. "After we unblocked Knox's root chakra—which took a great deal of time because of his tight-ass tendencies—he got an *erection!*"

This theatrical announcement was met with a mass

of delighted oohs and aahs and a spattering of applause.

Savannah clasped her hands together excitedly and looked meaningfully around at everyone. "It lasted for almost *two whole minutes!*"

She was evil, Knox thought as he felt his face flame with embarrassment. Evil. And he would make her pay. With a grand show of delighted support, Savannah grabbed hold of his arm and pressed close to him. "I'm so very proud of you, baby."

Edgar and Rupali beamed at him. "That's indeed something to be proud of, Knox. Congratulations on your erection."

Knox had been congratulated for many things over the years, but he could truthfully say that having a man congratulate him on an erection was a wholly new experience. A couple of the truly impotent men glared enviously at him.

"Er, thank you," he muttered self-consciously.

Beside him, Savannah sighed with sublime satisfaction, the faux picture of wifely adoration.

Rupali threaded her fingers through her husband's. "This is precisely why we have opened our home and hearts, why we decided to start this clinic. So that impotent men like Knox can come and reclaim their masculinity. With harmony and truth healing and the art of tantric ritual, perhaps he will be able to surpass even this breakthrough and lead his lover to climax." She gave Savannah an enigmatic look. "I don't think your problem lies in the lower chakras, Barbie. You will learn what I mean, and I would appreciate your telling me when it happens.''

Looking somewhat startled, Savannah merely nodded. Now what did Rupali mean by that? Knox wondered. After a moment, he leaned over and asked Savannah.

She shook her head, clearly bewildered. ''I have no idea.''

''Well, tell me when it happens. I want to know, too.''

''Oh, hell, Knox, you know as well as I do that nothing is going to happen.''

''Now how would I know that?'' he replied sardonically. ''Just think about me and my whopping two-minute erection.''

She had the nerve to laugh. ''Save your indignation. After this morning, you deserved it.''

''I wasn't the only one copping a feel,'' Knox replied, somewhat miffed. ''And I wasn't the one who was so horny I had to masturbate during my bath to get some relief.''

Her head jerked around and her stunned gaze found his.

''Yeah, that's right,'' he said with a crafty grin. ''I know.''

He had to give her credit—she recovered well. She blew out a disbelieving breath. ''Don't be ridiculous. Honestly, Knox, the size of your ego never ceases to amaze me. I—''

''It wasn't the size of my ego that sent you into

the bathroom and had you slipping your finger into—"

"Shut up," she said, squeezing her eyes tightly closed.

Knox tapped his finger thoughtfully against the chin. "Come to think of it, I think that was a violation of the rules. Perhaps I should report *your* climax—seeing as you're frigid and that would be a breakthrough," Knox threatened. "Then the whole room could applaud you and celebrate your orgasm."

"I'm sorry," she hissed.

"What?"

"I'm sorry, dammit."

He eyed her, his gaze lingering on her guarded expression. "Just what exactly is the problem?" Knox wanted to know, serious now. "What have I done—besides making you do this story—that has you alternately assaulting my character and my ego?" *Why don't you like me?* he demanded silently. *Why can't I charm you? For the love of God, why do I even care?*

She swallowed. "Nothing. It's my problem, not yours."

Oh, no. That was the closest thing to a personal admission she'd ever made and he had no intention of letting her get away with not finishing the thought. *"What is it?"* he pressed.

"We don't have time to go into this right now," Savannah hedged. She tucked her hair behind her ears. "Trust me, it's nothing. You're right. I've been unfair."

"If it was nothing, you wouldn't want to go for my throat every time the opportunity presented itself. Spill it, Savannah. I've got a right to know."

"Y-you remind me of someone, that's all."

"I remind you of someone," Knox repeated. "Who?"

Seemingly embarrassed, she huffed a breath and refused to look at him.

"A guy?" Knox guessed, annoyed beyond reason.

"Yes," she finally relented. "A guy. Are you happy now?"

No, he wasn't. He was anything but happy. "If I remind you of a guy and it's not a good thing, then one could logically deduce that this particular guy was a bastard who broke your heart. Am I right?"

"He did not break my heart," Savannah insisted icily. "I hadn't given him my heart to break."

No, only her trust, Knox realized, which any moron should have realized was almost as precious as her heart. "Do I look like him?"

"No."

"Do I act like him?"

Her shoulders slumped with an invisible weight. "I'd made myself believe that you did. But you don't."

Knox scowled, hopelessly confused. "If you no longer believe I act like him, then what's the problem?"

She emitted a low, frustrated growl. "Being here with you, this whole workshop..." She gestured wildly. "How am I supposed to stay out of the bathroom," she said meaningfully, "and not do what I—"

"Masturbate?"

"—did, when I'm here with *you* and we're surrounded by sex, sex and more sex?" Her voice climbed. "How am I supposed to think about anything else with all this talk of orgasms and erections and—"

Understanding suddenly dawned and Knox felt a self-satisfied grin spread across his lips. "You want me."

She shot him a dark look. "I didn't say that."

Something warm and tingly moved through his rapidly swelling chest. *"You want me."*

She paused. "Don't look so proud of yourself. I'd want just about anybody under the circumstances."

"Yeah...but you're not here with *anybody*. You're here with *me*."

"Brilliant deduction, Einstein."

"Would it make you feel any better if you knew I was having the same problem?"

She snorted. "Don't lie. You've already told me that the reason you brought me here was because you *weren't* attracted to me."

"Things have changed."

"Yes, I'm sure they have. You're a man and you've decided to make do with whomever is available. Which happens to be me. Meanwhile, neither one of us has any business being attracted to the other because we're here to do a job. And we can't truly do that job correctly unless we have sex, so it really is a screwed-up conundrum, isn't it, Knox?''

Another thought surfaced and suddenly everything became clear. ''Ahh,'' Knox said with a knowing twinkle. ''You wanted me *before* we left Chicago. That's why you didn't want to come. That's why you were so determined not to attend this workshop with me.''

''Keep this up, you cocksure moron. You're quickly losing your appeal.''

Savannah promptly stood and followed the rest of the group to the classroom, leaving Knox to glow with her revelation.

Savannah Reeves wanted him…and apparently always had. What to do with this new information? Knox wondered. Just exactly what the hell was he supposed to do? She'd told him for a reason—she hadn't just dropped this little bomb without some inkling of the consequences.

Did she expect him to be a hero and abstain, or was she simply putting the ball into his court? Did she want him to take the sexual lead, so that any blame could be laid squarely on him when this weekend was over?

Knox didn't know, but he knew he'd better figure it out. Otherwise, he feared he might single-handedly be responsible for Savannah never trusting a man again.

9

———

SAVANNAH COULDN'T BEGIN to imagine what had possessed her to all but admit that she'd been lusting after him for a year, but once the burn of humiliation cooled, she knew she'd undoubtedly feel better. It would be a relief not to have to pretend that she didn't want him. Since he'd deduced what had occurred during her bath last night, Savannah thought with a rueful grin, she hadn't been doing such a great job of pretending otherwise anyway.

He'd seen right through her.

The only reason she'd been able to hide the truth as long as she had was because she'd made a point of avoiding him.

But she couldn't avoid him here.

He was everywhere.

In her mind, in her mouth, beneath her hands, in her room, even in her bed.

Everywhere.

She couldn't escape him and was rapidly losing her resolve to try. The attraction had simply become bigger than she could handle, more than she could conceivably take on. She'd been doomed from the moment Chapman, the vengeful bastard, had forced her to come on this ill-conceived trip. No, Savannah thought with a dry chuckle, she'd been doomed from the moment she'd met Knox. It had all been simply a matter of time before she'd fall victim to his lethal appeal and her equally lethal attraction.

Knox sat down on the padded mat next to her. The hairs on her arms prickled at his nearness, seemingly drawn like a lodestone to him. For reasons she didn't dare dwell on, all of the chairs had been removed from the room and had been ominously replaced with big cushy mats.

"Have they started yet?" Knox whispered low.

God, she even loved the sound of his voice. It was deep and smooth and moved over her like an old blues tune. Could she get any more pathetic? "Not yet," Savannah finally managed.

Confusion cluttered his brow. "What are the mats for?"

"Dunno." *And don't care to speculate,* Savannah thought.

Knox glanced idly around the room. "Well, at least we know they aren't going to ask us to do it yet. That doesn't happen until tomorrow."

Tomorrow. The word hung between them and conjured a combined sense of anticipation and doom. Savannah didn't dare let herself think about what would happen tomorrow afternoon after they'd completed their so-called tantric-lovemaking training, and were sent to their room armed with that knowledge and a long night ahead of them. She supposed they should work on the story that they'd come here to get, but without actually having tried tantric sex to see if it truly worked, she didn't know how exactly they were supposed to do that.

When they'd first arrived, doing a fair article without participating in tantric sex seemed plausible. Now it didn't, and she could no longer tell if that idea was a product of journalistic integrity or sheer unadulterated lust. Probably a combination of both, Savannah decided.

With a sexy curl of his lips, Knox shifted on his mat and leaned closer to her. "I know this is going to sound strange," he confided, "but I'm starting to like this *kurta*. It's extremely comfortable. Feels good. I like being…unrestricted."

Savannah felt her lips twitch and tried not to think of which part of him was so friggin' unrestricted. Clearly he'd decided to torture her with his new information. His effort was redundant—she couldn't possibly want him any more. "It's a progressive-thinking man who can admit that he likes wearing a dress."

"It's not a dress," Knox corrected amiably. "It's a *kurta,* and if they have them in the gift shop, you can bet your sweet ass I'm buying one and taking it home."

Savannah chuckled drolly. "If you wear it anywhere but at home, I would strongly advise you to put on some underwear." She looked pointedly—

longingly—at his crotch. "Your entire package is plainly visible through the fabric."

"So is yours," he murmured suggestively. "Tell me, is that little star-shaped thingy on your right butt cheek a mole or a birthmark?"

He'd studied her ass that closely, eh? Swallowing her surprise, Savannah said, "It's a birthmark."

He nodded thoughtfully. "I thought as much."

Before Savannah could ponder that enigmatic comment any longer, the Sheas stood before the class and called order to the room.

"This morning we're going to teach some of the finer points of erotic massage," Edgar said. "Now, so that you understand the difference, erotic massage and genital massage aren't the same thing. We will cover those genital areas that bring such pleasure tomorrow, in *Love His Lingam* and *Sacred Goddess Stimulation.* I'm sure you are all looking forward to that," Edgar said with a small smile.

"What we're going to show you today, however," he continued, "will be how to heighten full-body awareness to bring ultimate pleasure. There are other areas of our bodies that enjoy touch. Our faces, for instance. Which is where we'll begin. We'll take our time about this, so that both partners can enjoy the exercise. To get the full enjoyment of this lesson, the receiver should be nude; however, we will leave that option up to each of you." He smiled encouragingly. "Men, you shall be givers first."

Nude? Savannah thought frantically as the couples

around them swiftly began to disrobe, including the Sheas. Savannah watched in fascinated horror as Edgar and Rupali casually slipped out of their *kurtas*.

"Givers sit crossed-legged and cradle your receiver's head in your lap," Edgar said.

Knox shrugged loosely, heaved a resigned breath and moved to draw his *kurta* over his head. He wore the slightest, sexiest grin, and those slumberous dark green eyes glinted with wicked humor and hidden sin.

"What the hell are you doing?" Savannah hissed, her heart beating wildly in her chest. "You don't have to get undressed. Clothing is optional."

"And I'm opting to come out of it." His lips tipped into a slow, unrepentant grin. "When I'm the receiver, I don't want anything between your hands and my skin."

His words sent gooseflesh skittering across her own skin. Nevertheless, unreasonable though it may be, she only wanted him naked with her. Not with a roomful of observers. A wee bit possessive, but she couldn't help herself. Her eyes narrowed. If even one of these sexually repressed sluts so much as looked at him, she'd break their fingers.

"Then you can be nude in our bedroom," she said icily. "But not here."

He paused, something shifted in his gaze and he smiled knowingly. "Ah, so you want me nude all to yourself?"

Did he have to be so arrogantly perceptive? Savannah thought with a stab of irritation. Was she that transparent? "What I want is for you to leave your clothes on," she told him, struggling to keep her patience.

"Knox? Barbie? Is there a problem?" Rupali asked.

To Savannah's continued mortification, the whole nude room turned to stare at them. "Uh, no. We're fine, thanks."

"There is no shame in flaunting our nude bodies," Rupali said with that misty tone. "We were created to delight in their perfect design. The human form is art in motion. You will find no judging eyes here." With a melancholy smile, she gestured to herself. "My own body is growing old and wrinkled. My breasts aren't as firm as they used to be, nor my stomach as flat." She straightened. "But I am proud, because this is the body I live in, and I am beautiful to myself."

Savannah envied the woman's confidence. In an age where the words *thin* and *youthful* defined beauty, Rupali could look at herself and feel imperfect but proud. How often had Savannah looked into the mirror and thought, *If only my breasts were larger? If only my thighs were thinner?*

Be that as it may, she was still just modest enough not to want to get naked in front of a roomful of strangers. Savannah summoned a wobbly smile. "I-I'd prefer to stay dressed."

Rupali nodded. "As you wish."

Everyone settled into the required position at Edgar's instruction. "Let's begin with a scalp massage," Edgar told them. "Be sure and ask your receiver what feels good to her. What she likes. Learn what makes your lover feel good and commit it to memory. Trust me," Edgar laughed. "You will reap the benefits of your effort tenfold."

Knox slid his fingers into her hair and began to knead her scalp with strong little circling movements. Savannah couldn't help herself, the audible moan of pleasure slipped past her smiling lips before she could stem it.

"Like that, do you?" Knox asked. She'd closed her eyes, but could hear the humor in his voice.

"Indeed, I do," she sighed softly.

Savannah had always enjoyed having her hair washed at her hairdresser's, had always found it relaxing, but she couldn't begin to compare that crude rubdown to the sensation of having Knox's warm, blunt-tipped fingers manipulating her tense scalp. The light scratch of fingernails, the strong press of his fingertips swirling over her head, lulled her. He caressed every inch from her hairline at her forehead, to the very nape of her neck, where tension had the tendency to gather. She hadn't anticipated this to be such an erotic experience, but a warm sluggish heat had begun to wind through her seemingly boneless body, proving her wrong.

"Let's move on, class," Edgar said, to Savannah's supreme disappointment. "Givers, move your attention to your receiver's face. So much emotion, so much feeling is transmitted through the muscles of our face. Consider the smile and the frown. These muscles, too, need attention. Caress your lover's face, and, remember, be sure to ask her what she likes,'' Edgar reminded. "Watch for what makes her feel good.''

Savannah smothered a sigh of satisfaction when she felt Knox's big warm hands cradle her face, felt them slide over her cheeks as he mapped the contours of her face. He smoothed his fingers over her closed lids, slid a thumb over the curve of her eyebrow, down her nose. *Heavenly,* she thought as another smile inched across her lips.

Knox brushed the back of his hand down the slope of her cheek. That move was more tender, more reverent, and somehow more personal than the others. Savannah longed to open her eyes, to look into his, and see if she could discover any inkling of his present thoughts, but the idea was no sooner born than abandoned, because Knox suddenly slid his thumb over her bottom lip.

Savannah had the almost irresistible urge to arch her neck, open her mouth and suck that thumb. She so desperately wanted to taste him that any part would do, and this particular part was most readily available. She settled for licking her lips after his finger had moved on, searching for even the smallest lingering hint of him.

To her immense gratification, she heard the breath

stutter out of Knox's lungs, felt a slight tension creep into his touch. He shaped her face once more with his hands, slid them down her arched throat and back up and around again. His touch grew slower yet more deliberately sensual. Savannah struggled to keep her breathing at a normal respiration, but it was getting considerably more difficult with each passing second.

Desire weighted her limbs and something hot and needy unfurled low in her belly, arrowed toward her wet and pulsing sex. She pressed her legs together and bit back the urge to roll over, scale his magnificent body and impale herself on the hard throbbing length of him.

If he could turn her into a quivering lump of lust with a scalp and face massage, just exactly how would she manage to control herself when he moved on to other erogenous zones? She wouldn't be able to bear it, Savannah decided. She simply—

"Before we continue," Edgar said, interrupting Savannah's turbulent thoughts, "let's change positions. Both the men and women need to find out how it feels to touch and be touched."

"Couples tend to get carried away as this lesson progresses," Rupali chimed in with a dry chuckle. "Please go ahead and change positions."

A reprieve, Savannah thought, profoundly relieved. As she sat up, she glanced at Knox and her gaze tangled with his. His eyes were dark and slumberous and a knowing, self-satisfied twinkle danced in those wickedly arousing orbs. The wretch knew exactly what he'd been doing to her, knew that he'd lit a fire in her loins that only a blast from his particular *hose* would put out.

Savannah narrowed her eyes into a look that promised retribution and more. Nobody set her on fire, then failed to get burned.

He would pay. With pleasure.

KNOX HAD SEEN that look in Savannah's eye before and knew it boded ill, undoubtedly for him. A flush of arousal tinged her creamy skin and her eyes were as hot as a blue flame. He'd known what he'd been doing to her during that massage, known that he'd lit her up.

Who would have ever thought that something as simple as a scalp and face massage could ignite such a blazing fuse of sexual energy? He'd listened to her little purrs of pleasure, felt her alternately go limp with relaxation and then vibrate with tension.

It had been the most singularly erotic sensation Knox had ever had.

Knox had been sexually active since his early teens. His sexual experiences had run the gamut of the highly romantic, to the down and dirty, and all species in between. He'd been drizzled in chocolate and licked clean, had eaten grapes from the pale pink folds of a woman's sex, had done it in a cab, in an elevator, and once in the bathroom of his dentist's office.

Yet, for all of his vast experience, nothing had

prepared him for the complete and total, all-consuming need he felt for Savannah. With each touch he'd become more aroused, more hungry for her. Feeling the delicate planes of her face beneath his hands, the soft swell of those lush lips, the sweet curve and soft skin of her cheek beneath his knuckles…

Something had happened to him in that instant, something so terrifying that Knox didn't dare name it, much less contemplate it. He'd looked at that beautiful, serene face of hers, that mess of bed-head curls, and a curious emotion had swelled in his chest, pushed into his throat and had forced him to swallow. His hands had actually trembled.

The picture she'd made in that instant was indelibly imprinted in his mind. No matter how much she blared and blustered, no matter how much blue sleet she slung in his direction, Knox would always remember the way she'd looked right then. She didn't know it yet, but she'd never be able to freeze him out again.

"Okay," Rupali said. "Let's begin."

Savannah leaned over him and smiled. "Let me know if I hurt you."

Oh, hell.

She slid her small fingers into his hair and rolled his scalp in little circles, front to back and side to side, alternating pressure with light touches and firmer kneads until Knox heard a long, decidedly happy growl of approval and realized it had come from the back of his own throat. She skimmed her fingers over the sensitive skin behind his ears, tunneled them into the thick hair at his nape. She scratched and massaged, kneaded and rubbed. Unexpected pleasure eddied through him and, though he imagined Edgar and Rupali would think that he'd totally missed the point of this exercise, it didn't take long for Knox to decide that those talented little fingers could be put to better use south of his navel.

He was a man, after all. He wouldn't be satisfied until her hand was wrapped around his throbbing rod, pumping him until he exploded with the force of his climax.

Still, Knox thought, as Savannah's fingertips slid through his hair once more, this was nice. Perhaps Edgar was onto something with all this erotic massage stuff. Every muscle was languid and relaxed, save for his dick—hell, he could do a no-hands push-up, he was so friggin' hard right now.

"Are you planning on hosting a party down there?" Savannah leaned down and asked him.

Knox slowly opened his eyes. "What?"

She was smiling one of those secret little smiles that made Knox feel as if he'd been caught with his fly down. "Are you planning on having a party down there?" She glanced pointedly at his groin. "You've erected quite a tent."

"Not a party," Knox told her silkily. "An intimate dinner for one. You hungry?"

Her eyes narrowed and then she licked her lips suggestively. *"Starving."*

If he hadn't been exercising tremendous control, Savannah would have turned him into the premature ejaculator she'd claimed he was with that little dramatic display.

"Givers," Rupali said, "move on to your receiver's face. Remember to note what pleases your lover."

"Would you like to know what pleases your lover, Savannah?" Knox murmured. "Would you like me to tell you?"

She swallowed and he felt her fingers tremble against his cheek. "I don't have a lover."

"That can be easily remedied."

She laughed softly, swept her fingers over his brow, down his cheek and along his jaw. "You wouldn't say these things if there was any blood left in your head."

Knox laughed. "If I'm not mistaken, *all* of it's in my head."

"Not the one that is responsible for logical thinking." She pressed a couple of fingers against his lips. "Shut up, Knox. People are starting to stare."

"Let 'em. I'm like Rupali. I'm proud. Besides, I've got something to prove." He grinned. "I'm going to break my two-minute erection record."

She tsked regretfully and massaged his temples. "Sorry, can't let that happen. Someone must protect our cover."

"Baby, you can't stop me."

"Wanna bet?"

Knox stilled and looked up at her. Clearly she hadn't gotten it yet, and wasn't going to until he spelled it out for her. "Savannah, my head is in your lap, inches away from the part of you that I want more than my next breath, and your hands might be on my face—which feels lovely, by the way—but in my mind, your hands are wrapped—along with your lips—around my rod and I'm seconds away from coming harder than I ever have in my life." He paused and let that sink in, watching her expression waver between determination and desire. His gaze held hers. "There is absolutely nothing you can say that's going to make me lose this erection."

A long, pregnant pause followed his blunt soliloquy. She blinked drunkenly for a second, then recovered and said four words that were guaranteed to make any hetero male lose even his most valiant erection.

"Chuck's whacking off again."

"Aw, Savannah," Knox woefully lamented. With a wince of regret, he squeezed his eyes shut but couldn't force the image away. The ick factor of Chuck and his happy hand swiftly deflated Knox's prized hard-on.

"And the big top comes down," Savannah whispered dramatically.

Knox opened his eyes and glared at her with amused accusation. "You are evil."

She smiled with faux modesty. "I try."

Knox felt a silent laugh rumble deep in his chest. "I'm sure you do."

A comfortable silence ensued, broken only by the soft sighs of pleasure that ebbed through the room. Savannah continued her sweet assault upon his face, gently massaging him. He'd let his lids flutter closed, but could feel the kiss of her gaze examining his every feature, measuring the muscle and bone against her hands. He heard a poignant, almost resigned sigh slip past her lips and wondered just what heavy realization she had come to. What he'd give to have even a glimpse into those thoughts.

Just as Knox was truly beginning to relax, Rupali interrupted the sensual play with more instructions. The givers and receivers were once again directed to change positions.

"We will massage backs and bellies, rumps and thighs, calves, insteps and even the smallest toe," Rupali told them. "No part of our bodies—aside from our genitals—shall be overlooked."

"You will know your lover's body better than your own by the end of this day," Edgar chimed in. "You will know what he or she likes, and you will discover neglected areas of your own body that bring pleasure when touched. Think of your lover's body like a musical instrument. Her sighs, her moans of pleasure, are your music, her quivers your applause."

"Women, the same holds true for you," Rupali shared. "Every indrawn breath, every expression of pleasure, every guttural growl from your man is his own primal music. While learning how to play your man, and while you, in turn, are played, your inner harmony begins to take form. The voice of your one-being will become clearer." She paused. "Seek that place, class. *Kundalini*," she emphasized. "Combined life force and sexual energy. Once you have experienced it, nothing else will ever suffice."

Knox whistled low, and he and Savannah shared a look. Her beauty, the absolute perfection of her face, struck him once more and the desire to reach out to slide his fingertips over those smooth features almost overpowered him.

Once you have experienced it, nothing else will ever suffice.

Knox grimly suspected those words held a double meaning for him. After Savannah...no one else would ever do.

10

———

THOUGH IT TOOK a monumental amount of restraint, Savannah limited her bath to just that—a bath. She and Knox had managed to make it from class back to their room after the all-day erotic massage session and, though her limbs had quaked and were limp as noodles, and her loins had been locked in a pit of permanently aroused despair, she'd managed to survive without begging him to plunge into her and put her out of her sexually frustrated misery.

Her only consolation was that Knox had been mired in that pit as well and, quite honestly, had not fared as well as she. Savannah's lips quivered. Her nipples didn't quite cause the stir his prominent erection did. When Knox was aroused, everyone knew it, could hardly fail to notice. She hated to dwell on it so, but Savannah couldn't seem to conquer her fascination with his enormous…article.

Neither could anyone else, for that matter, a fact that both annoyed and delighted her. For all intents and purposes of this workshop, that colossal penis was *hers* and hers alone. Both men and women alike gazed at them with envy, the men at Knox because they longed to be equally blessed, and the women, like her, were most likely astounded at the sheer size of him. Savannah enjoyed the being envied part—it was their greedy gazes lingering on her borrowed penis that pissed her off.

She'd heard a couple of the women talking about the phenomenon on the way out. "Pity he can't keep it up longer than two minutes though," one had said regretfully and to Knox's extreme embarrassment. During that session, his problem had seemed genuine to all. Every time that sucker had stood at attention longer that it should, Savannah had whispered the magic words, and *poof!* it would disappear. The magic words being, "Chuck's whacking off again." Cruel, she knew, but not any more cruel than what she'd suffered.

If she possessed even a shred of sanity by the time this workshop was over, Savannah would consider herself extremely lucky.

The evening ahead would undoubtedly be as trying as this day had been. As soon as she'd mentioned taking a bath, Knox had proclaimed it an excellent idea, and had once again tried to come out of that damned *kurta*. Truthfully, Savannah would have liked nothing better than to have taken him up on the idea, would have liked nothing better than to have had his hot, hard wet body wrapped around and pulsing inside hers. The tub had been designed for sin and so had his body and she wanted it more desperately with each passing second.

Quite honestly, Savannah didn't have a clue what they were supposed to do now. She'd laid all her cards on the table, and she supposed Knox had, too. He'd admitted that he wanted her now, and it was the *now* that kept messing with her head, the *now* that she was having trouble getting past.

A part of her wanted to say, *Consequences be damned, you've wanted him forever, here's your opportunity, just go for it already!*

But another part hated knowing that he *hadn't* wanted her to begin with, that it had taken a sex workshop for him to consider her attractive, and she seriously suspected her newfound appeal had more to do with convenience than actual interest. If she gave in to her baser needs and rode him until his eyes rolled back in his head as she so very much wanted to do, would she regret it later? Or would she regret it more if she didn't?

Savannah didn't know and, luckily, wouldn't have to decide until tomorrow...provided she didn't expire from longing first.

Knox rapped on the bathroom door, startling her. "The food's here. Come feed me."

A wry grin curled her lips as she opened the bathroom door. "I should let you starve," she told him.

"Why?"

"Just for the hell of it."

He shivered dramatically. "Chilly, chilly." That verdant green gaze was shrewd and glinted with humor. "You must not have had as much fun in the tub this evening. Don't worry, I can cure what ails you.'' His voice was low, practically a purr, and it sent a flurry of sensation buzzing through her.

She'd just bet he could, Savannah thought with a mental ooh-la-la. Did she have a prayer of resisting him? she wondered with furious despair.

After everything else they'd been through over the past twenty-four hours, feeding each other seemed downright tame. They spoke little during the meal, just systematically fed each other the tender strips of Hawaiian chicken, green beans, and macaroni and cheese, the latter being particular messy and involving a lot of cleanup.

Which meant a great deal of licking and sucking, and tongue in general.

Presently, a couple of Savannah's fingers were knuckle deep in Knox's hot mouth, and he'd decided to make a grand spectacle of getting her clean. He slid his tongue along her finger and alternately nibbled and sucked. Soft then hard, slow and steady, and, all the while, his heavy-lidded gaze held her enthralled.

Initially Savannah had managed a mocking smile, but she gloomily suspected it had lost its irreverent edge and had been replaced by a stupidly besotted grin. Her pulse tripped wildly in her veins and the desire that had never fully receded came swirling through like a riptide, washing away reason and rationale and anything that closely resembled common sense.

Knox finally commenced his cleaning and released her tingling fingers. "Savannah…can I ask you something?"

She blinked, still wandering in a sensual fog. "Sure."

"Where are you from?" he asked lightly. "Where did you grow up?"

The fog abruptly fled. Savannah suppressed a sigh and took a couple of seconds to shore up her defenses and decide how she should respond. She'd known that he'd ask—she'd watched the very questions form in his mind. Perhaps if she told him enough to satisfy his curiosity, he'd leave well enough alone. One could hope, at any rate.

Savannah pushed her plate away. "I grew up in lots of different places."

"Military?"

She blew out a breath. "No…foster care. My parents died when I was six."

Knox winced. "Oh. Sorry." He looked away. "Damn, I—"

Savannah hated this part. It was the same scenario every time. As soon as she told someone about her parents, they always apologized and then lapsed into an uncomfortable silence. She'd secretly hoped Knox would be different, but—

"That sucks, Savannah," Knox finally said. He plowed a hand through his hair, clearly out of his comfort zone, and his concerned gaze found hers. "I know that sounds so lame, but damn…that just really sucks.''

No points for eloquence, Savannah thought as her heart unexpectedly swelled with some unnamed emotion, but he definitely scored a few points for the blunt, wholly accurate summation. ''Thank you. You're absolutely right.'' She smiled, blew out a stuttering breath. ''It did suck.''

He arched a brow, leaned down and casually rested his elbows on his knees and let his hands dangle between his spread thighs. ''No family you could have gone to live with?''

''No,'' Savannah replied with a shake of her head, shoving the old familiar hurt back into the dark corner of her heart where she kept it. ''There was no one. We were a family of three and they died…and then there was me.''

''No brothers or sisters?''

''Nope.'' Time for her part of the interview to be over, Savannah decided, drawing in a shaky breath. She smacked her thighs. ''No more questions, Knox…unless you want to answer a few of mine.''

He smiled and lifted one heavily muscled shoulder in an offhanded shrug. ''Go ahead. Shoot. My life is an open book.''

We'd just see about that, wouldn't we? Savannah thought. ''Why do you work so hard at looking like you don't work hard?''

His affable mask slipped for half a second, and if

she hadn't been watching closely, she would have missed it altogether. "What?"

Savannah leveled him with a serious look. "I've watched you. I used to think that everything just came so easily to you…but I was wrong. You work very hard at your job, yet you make it a point to look like you don't." She paused. "Why is that, Knox?"

He looked away. "I don't know what you're talking about."

"The hell you don't. Be honest."

Knox swallowed. "Do you want the truth?"

"No," she deadpanned. "Tell me a lie. Of course, I want the truth!"

He smiled at that, then looked away once more. "It's simple, really. Everyone expects me to fail, and I don't want anyone to know just how much I want to succeed." He laughed self-consciously. "There you have it. My big dark secret."

He was right. It was simple, and yet more meaning and explanation lurked in that one telling sentence than she could have hoped for. Another thought surfaced.

"What do you mean *everyone?*" she asked.

Another dry humorless laugh rumbled from his chest. "Just what I said—everyone. Parents, co-workers, they all expect it." He passed a hand wearily over his face. "My parents keep waiting for me to come and work with my father, and so does everyone at the *Phoenix.* No one realizes that I'm not going anywhere, that I've chosen my career." His determined, intent gaze tangled with hers. "I'm a journalist. This is who I am, what I do. Does that make sense?"

Regret twisted her insides. Suddenly lots of things were beginning to make sense, Savannah thought, including the fact that she'd been no better than anyone else, if not worse. She'd taken one look at Knox, panicked, and had not gone to the trouble to look beyond her first impression, beneath the surface of his irreverent attitude. She'd formed the one uncharitable opinion and held fast to it, because she'd been too terrified to face the alternative.

Savannah swallowed. "It, uh, makes perfect sense. And Knox, for what it's worth, I think you're one helluva journalist."

His guarded expression brightened and dimmed all in the same instant. He looked away. "You're just saying that."

Savannah grinned at him. "Have you ever known me just to toss out a compliment?"

Those sexy lips tipped into an endearing smile. "No."

"Then the proper response is thank you."

He nodded. "Thank you."

The mood had become altogether too serious, Savannah decided. "We should get started on those chakras," she told him.

Knox winced, rubbed the back of his neck. "You're right. Do you mind if I grab a quick shower first?"

Savannah shook her head. "I need to organize my notes. We have a story to write, after all."

And she had some thinking to do…and a decision to make.

"I SWEAR I'LL CATCH YOU."

"I know that," Savannah said, exasperated.

"Then what's the problem?"

She speared her fingers through her hair and glared at him despairingly. "I can't let myself fall. I—I just can't do it. It's not a question of you being able to catch me—it's the whole idea of letting you. Don't you get it?"

Regrettably, he did, Knox thought. They'd been at this blind-trust test for the better part of thirty minutes and she still hadn't been able to let him catch her. Her reticence made perfect sense, now that she'd shared a little of her history.

Though Savannah had been very glib about the loss of her parents and her childhood, Knox had nonetheless glimpsed the little girl who'd felt abandoned beneath the woman who had learned to cope. Hell, no wonder she had trust issues. She'd had to learn to trust herself and no one else. She was completely alone. That wholly depressing thought had fully hit him while he'd been in the shower.

Savannah Reeves didn't have anyone.

Not a single living soul in this world to share her life with. Granted, his parents hadn't always supported him the way he would have liked…but at least they were there. Had provided the necessities and more to see him raised.

Savannah had gone through the foster-care system and apparently had come through the experience without so much as a mentor. If there had been any-body—anybody at all who'd made a difference in her life—she would have shared that. What she'd said had revealed a lot, but what she hadn't said revealed more.

In all truth, Knox could have waited to take his shower in the morning, but after listening to her re-signedly tell him about her parents, Knox had sud-denly been filled with self-loathing and disgust. He'd turned into the whiny little rich boy he'd always sworn he'd never become. So what if his parents didn't like his job? They'd get over it. So what if his co-workers at the *Phoenix* didn't respect him? He'd do his job to the best of his ability, and he'd *make* them, by God. He wouldn't leave them a choice.

When compared with the trials of Savannah's life, Knox's little letdowns had seemed petty, selfish and small. *He'd* felt small, and Knox had decided that the only way he could redeem himself was to become someone she respected…and someone she trusted.

Thus, he'd come out of his shower prepared to conquer her trust issues. Knox frowned. So far, it wasn't working.

''Okay,'' Knox finally said. ''Let's try something different. Face me and fall forward.''

Savannah heaved an impatient sigh. "This is pointless. I'm not—"

"Do it."

"Oh, all right." She moved to stand in front of him.

"Now look at me and fall."

She chewed anxiously on her bottom lip, fastened her worried gaze onto his and fell…right into his outstretched arms.

Knox grinned, unaccountably pleased. His mood lightened considerably. "Now that's more like it."

She smiled hesitantly. "It is, isn't it? Thanks, Knox. That was a good idea."

His chest swelled, amazed that he'd been able to impress her. "Okay, now let's try this. Stand with your side to me and fall."

She did, from both sides, and both times fell right into his arms.

"And now for the final test," Knox teased. "Let's try the blind-trust test again."

Savannah's hopeful smile warmed him from the inside out. She swallowed and nervously gave him her back. For half a second, Knox thought she would go for it, would take the proverbial plunge, but just short of letting gravity have its way, Savannah drew up short with a frustrated wail of misery.

"Why?" she railed with a whimper. "Why can't I do this?" Defeat rounded her shoulders and the breath left her lungs in a long, dejected whoosh.

Knox, too, felt the drag of disappointment.

"You'll get it," he encouraged. "You've definitely made some improvement."

"I know, and thank you." She shot him a sheepish look. "I don't mean to sound ungrateful. I just— I just *hate* to fail."

Knox summoned a droll smile. "I don't think anyone particularly cares for it."

Some of the tension left her petite frame and her lips twitched adorably. "I suppose not."

"Why don't we move on to the chakras? We're behind, you know." Knox strolled across the room and sprawled across the foot of the bed as he'd done the night before. He heaved a disgusted breath. "Marge and Chuck are beating us."

Savannah cast him a sidelong glance. "Humph. Mostly Chuck just beats himself."

Knox felt his eyes widen and a shocked laugh burst from his throat. He looked over at Savannah, pushing down his smile. "So, what's the next chakra we're supposed to unblock?" Knox asked innocently. He knew, of course. He simply enjoyed messing with her.

Her gaze twinkled with perceptive humor. "It's the genital chakra, which you well know," she added pointedly. She settled herself against the headboard, placed the book in her lap and opened it to the appropriate page. He watched her lips form the words as she read silently. After a moment, she looked up. "Well, now this is interesting. According to the book, this chakra can be one of the most difficult to deal with.''

''That being the case, should I get naked?''

''I think not.''

''Damn,'' Knox said with chagrin. ''Funny, but I distinctly remember you saying that I could be naked in our room.''

Though she refused to look at him, Knox discerned a slight quiver at the corners of her lips. ''I lied. Now shut up and listen.'' She paused and read some more. ''I—I don't think either one of us is blocked in this chakra.''

That figured. This was the only one he'd looked forward to working on. Knox scowled. ''Are you sure? I'm feeling a little blocked. I think that you should unblock me. Does it say how you're supposed to do that?''

Savannah poked her tongue in her cheek. ''Yes, as a matter of fact, it does.''

Anticipation rose. Knox turned over onto his back and laced his hands behind his head. ''Then do it.''

''Are you sure?'' she asked gravely.

Oh, was he ever. ''Yes, I'm sure.''

''Well, if you're sure.'' Knox felt the bed shift as she moved into a better position. ''You'll need to roll over.''

Something in her too innocent tones alerted Knox to the fact that all was not as it seemed. Obviously he wasn't going to get the hand job he'd been dreaming of. With a premonition of dread, he opened his closed eyes and glanced at her. Just as he suspected, mischief danced in that cool blue gaze. "Roll over?" he asked slowly. He dreaded asking, but knew he must. "Why?" he asked ominously.

"Because, according to my handy booklet, I'm supposed to unblock your root chakra while I'm unblocking your genital chakra." She smiled. "So why don't you—just try to relax and I'll—"

Realization dawned, and the semiarousal he'd enjoyed instantly vanished. His ass shrank in horrified revulsion. Knox slung an arm over his eyes. "Forget it," he growled.

"—make this as painless as possible." She paused. "What?" she asked innocently.

"Forget it."

"Are you sure? I'd be happy—"

"Savannah…" Knox warned. What was with the preoccupation with a person's ass? Knox wondered.

She laughed, not the least bit repentant. "I tried to tell you that we weren't blocked. Let's just chant the couples blessing and move on."

"What's that?" Knox asked, still perturbed.

Savannah aligned her body with his and Knox felt marginally better. She pillowed her head on the crook of her arm and held the book aloft with her other hand. Amusement glittered in her eyes and her lips were twitching with barely suppressed humor. "Okay, I'm supposed to say, 'I love you at your lingam and bless your wand of light.'" She promptly dissolved into a fit of giggles.

Knox laughed as well. "And what am I supposed to say?"

"You're supposed to say, 'I love you at your yoni and bless your sacred space.'"

How could people say this stuff with a straight face? Knox wondered. "Consider yourself loved and blessed," he said dryly. "Let's move on. What's next?"

Savannah sat up and wiped her eyes. "The belly chakra."

"Does my ass have anything to do with this one?" Knox asked suspiciously.

"Er…I don't think so."

He nodded. "Then continue."

"Okay, now this one is actually pretty interesting," Savannah said. "Our bellies are the feeling centers. Our emotions are energy in motion and tend to grow out of our bellies and take whatever path is appropriate for their expression."

Knox nodded thoughtfully. That did make a sort of strange sense. He considered his nudge. It definitely came from his belly. "That one seems almost plausible," Knox admitted.

Savannah's brow furrowed thoughtfully. "It does, doesn't it? Just think of butterflies in your belly, and nausea, and that sinking sensation when something isn't quite right. Gut reaction, gut feelings." She hummed under her breath, read a little more. "I can actually relate to this one. We're supposed to chant *ram* now."

"Ram," Knox deadpanned. "I'm unblocked, what about you?"

"Ram, it's a miracle, so am I."

Knox grinned. "Amazing, isn't it?"

She grinned adorably. "Without a doubt."

"What's next?"

Savannah flipped the page. Her eyes widened. "Ooh, the heart chakra. The center of love, courage and intimacy." Her brow wrinkled in perplexity. "A broken heart is most often the cause of a block in this chakra. We're supposed to share our hurts with each other to promote healing. It also says that a woman generally has to feel love in this chakra before she can experience sexual intimacy and that, likewise, a man must have sexual intimacy with a woman first in order to build trust." She snorted. "Hell, no wonder we're all screwed up. Men and women are completely opposite."

A bark of dry laughter bubbled up Knox's throat. "Was there ever a doubt?"

Savannah thwacked him with the book. "Pay attention. You're supposed to be telling me about all of your old heartaches."

"Sorry, I can't."

"Why not?"

"Because I don't have any."

Savannah raised a skeptical brow. "You've got to be kidding. You've never had your heart broken?"

"No," he sighed, "can't say that I have."

She paused. Swallowed. "Well, I don't know

whether to congratulate you, or offer my sympathies."

The confident smile Knox had been wearing slipped a fraction. "What do you mean *offer your sympathies?*"

The twinkling humor had died from her eyes and had been replaced with something mortifyingly like pity. "Well...that's just sad, Knox."

Knox blinked, astounded. "You think it's sad that I've never had my heart broken?" Was she cracked or what? he wondered, feeling a curious tension build in his chest.

Savannah sighed, seemingly at a loss to explain herself. Finally she said, "Not that you haven't had your heart broken, but that you've never been close enough to another person for it to have happened. Everybody needs their heart broken at least once."

He scowled. "I think I'll pass."

That soft sympathetic gaze moved over him. "You don't get it. It's what you're missing up until you get your heart broken that makes it all worthwhile."

"Is that the voice of experience talking?" Knox asked, mildly annoyed.

He didn't know why her words bothered him so much, but they did. His skin suddenly felt too tight and his palms had begun to sweat. What? Did she think him incapable of love? Did she think him too shallow for such a deep emotion? If he ever found the right person, he could love her, dammit. He was capable of loving someone. He'd simply not found anyone he wanted to invest that much emotion in, that's all. But it didn't mean he couldn't do it.

Savannah's gaze grew shuttered and she tucked her hair behind her ear, an endearingly nervous gesture. "Yes, it's the voice of experience. I've...almost had my heart broken."

"Almost?" Knox questioned skeptically.

"I'm still in denial."

"Oh. Well, I still wouldn't think it would be a pleasant ordeal," Knox replied drolly.

She smirked. "No, it wasn't."

"You should probably share this with me," Knox told her magnanimously, "seeing as we're supposed to heal old hurts to unblock this chakra."

She pinned him with a shrewd glare. "You have absolutely no interest in unblocking my heart chakra, you great fraud—you're simply curious."

Smiling, he shrugged. "There is that."

Savannah picked at a loose thread on her *kurta*, but finally relented with a sigh. "There was someone once," she admitted. "His, uh, parents didn't approve of me, though, so he broke up with me and went to Europe."

Knox abruptly sat up. *"What?"*

She laughed without humor. "It's true, I swear."

"What kind of a pansy-ass were you dating?" Knox asked incredulously.

She lifted her shoulders in a halfhearted shrug. "A spineless one with no class, as it turned out."

That summed it up nicely, Knox thought. What

sort of ignorant prick let his parents pick his girl-
friend? he wondered angrily, much less ditched Savannah for Europe? Hell, no wonder she didn't trust
anybody. No wonder she couldn't pass that blind-
trust test. When had anyone ever given her a reason
to trust them? When had anyone been worthy of it?

"I've had enough heart chakra healing," Savannah told him. "Let's move on. We're almost finished."

It took a considerable amount of effort, but Knox
finally forced his violent thoughts away and managed
to concentrate on the task at hand. "Sure. What's
next?"

"The throat chakra, the source of authentic expression." She chewed the corner of her lip and read
some more. "Okay, we're supposed to hear and heed
our inner voices, express our most dangerous emotions, even rage. But we have to learn to do this in
gentle tones with our lovers and save our loud voices
for when we're alone."

Knox nodded. "That's simple enough. We're not
supposed to scream at one another."

"Right. We're supposed to tell our truths and sing
our true songs, sanctify sex and choose words that
glorify our sexual organs, such as *sacred space,
wand of light*, etc...."

"Got it. What else?"

Her brow furrowed. "This is another one that sort
of makes sense. Communication flows through this

chakra. Think of some of the things that happen physically to you when you get upset.''

''Like what?'' Knox asked, not following.

''A lump in your throat, for instance. Or being too overcome to speak.''

He nodded. ''Makes sense. Anything else?''

Savannah glanced at the book. ''Uh…we're supposed to place our hand over each other's throats and tell each other to sing our true songs, then chant *ham*.''

Knox leaned forward and placed his hand over Savannah's slim throat. He grinned. ''Sing your true song, baby. *Ham*.''

Savannah reciprocated the gesture. ''Ditto.''

''How many more of these chakras do we have?'' Knox asked as he rolled back onto his side.

''Just two.''

''Okay.''

''Why? Do you want to quit for tonight?''

''No. We're going to need lots of time tomorrow night to work on *Love His Lingam* and *Sacred Goddess Stimulation*.'' And he couldn't wait.

Savannah pulled in a slow breath. ''Right,'' she all but croaked. ''Okay, the next one is the brow chakra, logic and intuition, the tird eye and all that. Think of people with psychic ability, or with a keen mind. Dreams and such. All of those things are a product of the brow chakra.''

Another one that was almost plausible, Knox thought, as possible angles for their story spun through his mind. His grandmother had been physic, so he knew such powers existed. "Are you blocked in that chakra?"

"No," Savannah said. "Are you?"

"No."

Another smile quivered on her lips. "Then we're supposed to join brows, stare at each other until our eyes seem to merge and say, "'I r-rejoice in how you comprehend and intuit.' Then we chant *ooo*."

Smiling, Knox rubbed the back of his neck. "You've got to be kidding."

"Nope," she said, tongue in cheek.

"Okay." Knox rolled himself into the center of the bed, then sat up on his knees. Savannah set the book aside and, mischief lighting her eyes, assumed the position as well. Gazes locked in mutual amusement, they leaned forward and their brows met.

"I feel utterly ridiculous," Savannah said, her sweet breath fanning against his lips. "What about you?"

"Most definitely."

The words were no sooner out of his mouth than an altogether different sensation took hold. Several sensations, in fact. The simultaneous registration of her sweet scent, the press of her body and the proximity of her lips hit him all at once. His heart thundered in his chest, pumping his blood that much faster to his groin. Fire licked through his veins, and he burned with the need to possess her, to lay her down, spread her thighs and bury himself so deeply into her that there would be no beginning and no end, just *them*.

Savannah's eyes darkened with desire, the heat burning away any vestiges of lingering humor. He could feel the quickened puff of her breath against his lips, heard her swallow.

Knox's blood roared in his ears, drowning out any would-be protests. He'd kissed her repeatedly since the beginning of this damned workshop, but it had always been at Edgar or Rupali's prompting. He hadn't taken the plunge and made the conscious decision to kiss her, taste her of his own accord. But he was making that decision now—he couldn't help himself—and he wanted her to know the difference and, more important, to feel it.

Knox gently cupped her face, held her gaze until his lips brushed lightly over hers. He hovered on a precipice, he knew, yet he didn't possess the power to keep from plunging headlong over it. Then his eyelids fluttered closed under the exquisite weight of some unnamed emotion…and he sighed…and eagerly embraced the fall.

11

SAVANNAH HAD KNOWN the moment that her brow touched his that she'd made a tactical error—she'd touched him. She knew, didn't she, that she couldn't touch Knox without melting like a Popsicle on the Fourth of July? She knew, and yet it hadn't made one iota of difference because she simply could not resist him. She had been inexplicably drawn to him from the moment she'd first seen him, had been lusting after him in secret torment every day since.

Just seconds ago, she'd watched the humor fade from his gaze, chased away by the power of a darker, more primal emotion. His entire body had grown taut, and then, as though he'd made some momentous decision, she'd discerned a shift in his posture. Then those amazing hands she'd imagined roaming all over her body in all sorts of wicked acts of depravity had cupped her face in a gesture so truly sweet she'd almost wept with the tenderness of it.

In the half second before his lips touched hers, Savannah realized the import of that soft touch, and her heart, along with the rest of her wayward body, had all but melted.

Knox Webber wanted her. *At long last.*

With a sigh of utter satisfaction, Savannah eagerly met his mouth, threaded her fingers through his hair and kissed him the way she'd always dreamed of kissing him. She poured every single ounce of belated desire into the melding of their mouths and was rewarded when Knox responded with a hungry growl of pleasure. The masculine sound reverberated in her own mouth, making her smile against his lips. His tongue slid over hers, plundered and plumbed, a game of seek and retreat that soon had Savannah's insides hot, muddled and quivering with want.

Knox molded her to him, slid those talented hands down her back and over her rump, and back up again. His hands burned a heated trail of sensation everywhere they touched and she longed to have them plumping her swollen breasts, sliding over her belly and lower, then lower still until his fingers worked their magic on the part of her that needed release most of all.

As though he'd read her mind, Knox smoothed his hand up her rib cage and cupped one pouting breast. She sagged under the torment of the sensation and, with a groan of satisfaction, Knox followed her down upon the bed. His warmth wrapped around her and the long, hot length of him nudged her hip.

She sucked in a harsh breath between their joined mouths and then sent her hands on their own little exploration of his body. The smooth, hard muscles of his shoulders, down the slim indention of his spine and back over the tautened sinews of his magnificently formed back.

Having mapped that terrain, she moved onto the sleek slope of his chest, the bumpy ridges of his abdomen, and over one impossibly lean hip. He was magnificent, the most perfectly put-together man she'd ever laid her greedy little hands upon. She claimed each perfection as her own. *Mine,* Savannah thought as she grasped his shoulders once more. *Mine,* she thought again as she slid her hand down his side. *Mine, mine, mine,* with each new part.

All mine.

Savannah winced as the *kurta* bunched annoyingly beneath her hungry hands. Knox had thrown one heavily muscled thigh across her leg and Savannah had the hem in her hand and had begun to swiftly tug it up his body before the significance of what she was doing surfaced in her lust-ridden brain.

Swallowing a cry of regret, she tore her mouth from his and pried his hand off her breast. "We can't…do this," she breathed brokenly.

Knox's lips curled in invitation and he nuzzled the side of her neck. "Oh, but we can," he told her. He tugged at the neckline of her *kurta,* attempted to bare her breast. "Come on, I'll show you mine if you show me yours."

Savannah dragged his head away from her neck and ignored the fizzle of warmth his wicked lips had created. Ignored his invitation to play a sexy game of show-and-tell. "Knox," she said desperately. "*Think.* We can't—"

"Thinking is overrated. In fact, you've told me repeatedly that I should try not to think. Remember? Something about it upsetting the delicate balance of my constitution." He bent his head and sucked her aching nipple into his mouth through the soft cotton fabric. The shock of pure sensation arched her off the bed and rent a silent gasp from her throat.

Sweet heaven.

Though it nearly killed her, Savannah wrenched his head from her breast. "Stop. We have to talk. We can't—"

"Talk?" Knox tsked and thumbed her nipple distractingly. "You know we can't talk for more than two minutes without arguing. This is a much more agreeable way to pass the time and you know it." He slid his fingers up her thigh and brushed her feminine curls.

Savannah bit her bottom lip and whimpered, resisted the urge to press herself against those teasing fingers. Knox took her hesitation as permission, and gently stroked her through the fabric.

She squirmed with need and her clit throbbed and her womb grew even heavier with want, but Savannah managed to stay his hand with a will born of stubborn desperation. "*Listen,* please," she insisted breathlessly. "We can't do this *now.*"

She watched Knox's sinfully sculpted lips ready a protest, but the *now* registered a second before he could push the sound from his lips. He arched a sulky brow. "What do you mean *now?*"

"The rule," Savannah reminded impatiently. "No sex until tomorrow night."

For better or for worse, she'd just told Knox Webber that she'd sleep with him tomorrow night, Savannah realized. She refused to consider anything beyond Sunday, anything that might remotely resemble second thoughts or regrets. She'd wanted Knox...forever. There was simply no other way for this weekend to end. She'd known the outcome, had known this would happen, the moment Chapman had commanded that she come to this workshop.

And, though it sounded like a lame excuse, at least they would know for sure if there was any real merit to the tantric way. They would be able to lend true credibility to their story.

That should please Knox, anyway, Savannah thought with a prick of regret. After all, that's what had brought them here.

"Are you saying what I think that you're saying?" Knox asked carefully. Desire tempered with caution glinted in that sexy green gaze.

Savannah swallowed tightly. "Yes, I am." She managed a shaky grin. "It's inevitable, right? And then there's the story to consider."

A shadow shifted over his face and he grew unnaturally still. "The story?"

"Right." Savannah shrugged out from under him and stood. "I mean, how can we really tell our readers if there is any truth to the whole concept of tantric sex if we don't try it?''

Knox stared at her for several seconds with a curiously unreadable look, then he abruptly smiled, but it lacked his typical humor. "You're right. We need to do it, we need to sacrifice ourselves, for the sake of the integrity of our story.''

There was subtle sarcastic tone to Knox's voice that needled Savannah. Honestly, she didn't think it would be that big a damned sacrifice. Clearly she'd said something that had pissed him off, but she didn't have a clue what that something could be. *Sacrifice?* she wondered again, even more perturbed. If she hadn't stopped him just a few minutes ago, they'd undoubtedly be enjoying the aftermath of an earth-shattering orgasm, and yet now—because he'd have to wait until tomorrow—he was sacrificing himself? Well, to hell with him, Savannah thought.

"I'm going for a walk," she said tightly, and headed for the door. She was embarrassingly close to tears.

"Savannah, wait," Knox said. He muttered a hot oath and pushed a hand through his hair. "I'm bungling this.''

She paused and turned around. "Bungling what?''

His tortured gaze met hers and held it. "If we make love here tomorrow night, it's not going to have anything to do with a damned story," he said heatedly. "At least, not for me. I want you, dammit—I want you more than anything—but it doesn't have anything to do with getting a story. And I certainly don't expect you, nor want you, to sleep with me for the sake of one. Do you understand?''

Something light and warm moved into her chest and swelled. She blinked, swallowed. ''I think I'm getting it.''

''Good.''

''I'm still going for a walk.''

He nodded.

Savannah opened the door, then paused. ''Just so you know,'' she said haltingly, ''it wouldn't have been about the story for me, either.'' Her wobbly smile made an encore appearance. ''It was only a face-saver, you know, in case you regretted things later.''

His steady green gaze rooted her to the floor with its intensity. ''I won't regret it.''

''Neither will I,'' Savannah murmured, and prayed fervently that statement proved to be true.

''DON'T WE NEED TO GET that last chakra out of the way before we go to breakfast?'' Knox asked. He didn't want anything besides *Love His Lingam* and *Sacred Goddess Stimulation* between him and Savannah after they wound up classes today.

''Yes, we do,'' she called from the bathroom. ''Just let me finish my hair and we'll go over it.''

Her hair, Knox thought with part chuckle, part snort. Well, he had several minutes then and he would use them to think about everything that had happened between him and Savannah last night. She'd cut her walk short—after catching Chuck and his hand making love on the front porch—and when she'd returned, they'd lain in the dark and talked and laughed until the wee hours of the morning.

They'd talked about everything from favorite soft drinks, to work, and a multitude of subjects in between. Had even managed to agree—after *much* discussion—on what angle to use for this story. Knox had picked up on a great deal of hostility between her and Chapman, but when he'd asked, naturally she'd clammed up and quickly changed the subject. Knox didn't know what had happened to create such animosity, but as soon as he returned to Chicago, he was determined to find out. If not from Savannah, then from a different source.

Journalists didn't come any finer, more professional, than Savannah Reeves. If there was a problem, undoubtedly it was on Chapman's end, not hers. And if that were the case, and Chapman had been treating her unfairly, he would soon be held accountable. Knox's hands involuntarily balled into fists. Boss or no, Chapman would pay.

Savannah finally emerged from the bathroom wrapped in a towel Knox mentally willed to fall off but, to his regret, didn't. Other than a hint of makeup and the fresh look of her, Knox could discern no significant difference. Her hair still looked as if it had been hit with a weed-whacker, then combed with a garden rake. He grinned. Adorably messy, as always.

Catching his smile, Savannah's steps faltered as she went to put her things into her overnight bag. "What are you smiling about?" she asked cautiously.

Knox rested his chin on his thumb and index finger. "Your hair," he replied honestly.

She rolled her eyes. "This is as good as it gets. If you're ashamed to be seen with me, I suggest you get over it."

"Who said anything about being ashamed? I like it."

She shot him a look. "Right."

"I do," Knox insisted. "It looks all messy, like you just rolled out of bed."

She heaved a resigned sigh. "Wow, Romeo. Is that supposed to be a compliment? Gonna write me an Ode to Bed Head?"

"Of course it's a compliment. Your normally quick wit seems a little sluggish this morning. Didn't you hear the part about the bed?"

"Yes, and I fail to see the relevance."

"Of course, you don't. You're not a man."

Savannah's lips curled. "Another brilliant observation. The power of your deductive reasoning astounds me."

"Aw, hell. Think for a minute, Savannah. If I look at you and think that you just look like you rolled out of bed, then what other things am I likely to think about?"

"Bad breath, drool, pillow creases—"

Knox chuckled. "You're thinking like a woman. Think—"

Her eyes widened in mock astonishment. "Imagine that."

"Come on. Think like a man," Knox told her.

Savannah shrugged. "I don't know. I—"

"Then I'll tell you. I'm thinking about what you were wearing in that bed. Do you sleep in the nude, in a T-shirt or a silk teddy? What have you been doing in that bed? Better yet, what could you do with me—or—to me in that bed? What would I do to you if I had you in bed? What would—"

"I've got it," Savannah interrupted, her face flushed. "You look at my hair and think about sex."

"Right."

"Knox, when do you look at a woman and *not* think about sex?"

"I've just paid you a compliment, right?"

"I suppose."

"Then the proper response is thank you," he said, reminding her of the proper compliment etiquette she'd been so quick to share with him.

A slow grin trembled into place. "Thank you."

"You're welcome." He smiled contentedly. "Now what about that crown chakra?"

Savannah pulled her *kurta* on over her head, tugged it into place and then shimmied out of the towel. What a dirty trick, Knox thought. He'd been nice enough to drop his towel for her and she couldn't show a little consideration and reciprocate the gesture? "I'll get the book," she said drolly. "You just sit there."

Knox frowned innocently. "What? What did I do now?"

"Couldn't you have gotten this book and gone over it yourself while I was getting ready?"

"No."

She looked taken aback at his simple, honest reply. "Why the hell not?"

"Because I've been thinking about having sex with you."

A shocked laugh burst from her throat and she flushed to the roots of her hair. She swallowed and seemed incapable of forming a reply. Speechless *and* blushing, Knox thought. Damn, he was good.

"The crown chakra," Knox prodded.

"Right." The tip of her tongue peeked from between her lips as she turned to the end of the booklet. "Okay," she began. "The crown chakra is the center of spiritual connectivity. Now that all of our chakras have been unblocked, we're supposed to imagine white light and lotus blossoms flowing from the tops of our heads." Savannah's twinkling gaze met his astounded one.

"What?"

"Lotus blossoms and light flowing from our heads." She twinkled her fingers above her head. "We're supposed to merge and inhale one another and feel in unity with the universe. We chant *mmm.*"

"Should we merge now or later?"

Her lips twitched. "Later. Come on, we're going to be late for breakfast."

Knox heaved an exaggerated sigh and reluctantly stood. "I'd rather inhale and merge with you."

"Later," she laughed.

He would take that as a promise.

"WELCOME TO THE long-awaited *Sacred Goddess Stimulation* class," Rupali said with a secret smile. "I know you have all looked forward to this, but, before we begin, I would like to take a moment to caution you about what you are about to see and hear in this particular class." She paused. "This is a very dramatic lesson, very graphic. There is simply no way to adequately show you how to perform these services for your lover without demonstrating them. You are welcome to practice on your lover during class, but your time would be best spent observing and learning from Edgar and me. If you are in any way going to be uncomfortable with what I have just explained, then you shouldn't be here."

Well, that ruled her out, Savannah thought. That huge map of a vagina sitting on the easel next to Rupali had, quite frankly, shocked the crap out of her. "Knox, I—"

"No."

Well, all righty then. Savannah settled back into her seat, and did her dead-level best to ignore the huge vaginal chart.

"Is there anyone who would like to leave this class?" Rupali asked.

Several headshakes and soft-spoken no's filtered through the room, assuring Savannah that they were all a bunch of perverts, herself included. She didn't know exactly what all *Secret Goddess Stimulation* entailed, but she strongly suspected that it would have been something better learned in the privacy of their room with a handy how-to video.

"Okay, then. Let's begin." Rupali looked to her husband and he stepped forward.

"Men, this class is about learning how to properly please your woman, what makes her feel good, what will bring her pleasure." His gaze lingered on the class at large for a moment, then he continued. "First, we're going to cover the basic anatomy of the female sex."

To Savannah's growing discomfort, Edgar pointed out all of the necessary female parts, lingering particularly on the clitoris, which he described as the pearl of sensation.

Edgar held up a glass jar—his *yoni* puppet—and demonstrated the proper way to find a woman's G-spot. He curled his ring finger and wiggled it back and forth. "Can everyone see? It's not the depth, the length, or the size which stimulates this concentration of sensitive cells, it's the positioning. Once you get it right, you'll be able to bring her to climax—possibly even ejaculation—every time you make love." He smiled. "And, yes, I said ejaculation. Though it's

known to be a rare occurrence in traditional intercourse, women can and do typically ejaculate during
tantric sex. Ah, I see a few skeptical faces in the
crowd. In just a few moments I will provide the proof
of that statement.''

Rupali laughed. "I think it is *I* who will be the
one providing the proof, darling.''

Savannah had to confess a degree of morbid fascination. She'd read about female ejaculation before,
but had never imagined she'd get to witness the phenomenon.

"Jesus," Knox breathed next to her.

"What's the matter?"

"I don't know if I can watch this," he said.

"What?" She swiveled to look at him. "I thought
this was the class that you'd been waiting for?"

A muscle worked in his tense jaw. "Yeah, but I
was wrong. I don't want to look at this woman's
yoni—I want to look at yours. This is too weird, too
cracked. It's like watching my parents."

"Well, it's too late now," Savannah hissed.
"We're stuck here. Just avert your eyes."

"Can't," Knox said. "It's like looking at a high-
way accident. You dread it, but you can't look
away."

"Well, try. It'll be over soon."

Knox startled her by sliding his hand in hers, sending a flush of delight and warmth straight to her rapidly beating heart.

It wasn't over soon—it lasted forever. Rupali and

Edgar were seasoned tantrics and believed in letting the class get their money's worth because, much to Knox and Savannah's horror, Edgar showed how to pleasure Rupali repeatedly. With his hand, his penis and a few battery-operated gadgets that Savannah had never seen. Several members of the class had decided to test their newfound knowledge during the session as well. So, not only did they get to see Rupali and Edgar's "sacred spaces" and "wands of light," they got to see several others, too.

In addition to those orgylike images, Rupali and Edgar made good on their promise—Rupali ejaculated. Knox had become increasingly miserable throughout the lesson, but seemed particularly disturbed by watching Rupali's *amrita*—or "sweet nectar"—arc through the air like a clear rainbow.

Soon after Edgar and Rupali announced a brief intermission for refreshments between classes. *Love His Lingam* would start momentarily.

"I want to go to the room," Knox whispered tightly.

"You don't want to participate in *Love His Lingam?*"

"No."

"Knox, I hesitate to bring this up, but you're the one who planned this trip and you're the one who wanted to do this story. I'm not remotely interested in going in here and learning how to blow you or give you a hand job—I can do that without any instruction and guarantee that you won't have any complaints. But if we're going to do this story the way we should, then you know we need to just suck it up and go.''

Knox grinned. "Suck it up, eh?"

She jabbed him. "You know what I mean," she said impatiently.

"Oh, all right," Knox finally relented. "But I am not going to like it," he growled.

"I didn't say you had to like it, I just said you had to suck it up."

"Only if you will, baby," Knox muttered. "Only if you will."

Savannah conjured a sexy grin, leaned forward and, to Knox's complete astonishment, stroked him through the *kurta* the way she'd been wanting to for the past forty-eight hours. "You can bet your sweet ass."

12

___

BY THE TIME Rupali had finished *Loving Edgar's Lingam*, Knox was in a shell-shocked, near-catatonic state. Sure he'd gleaned a few little tidbits of knowledge about his equipment that he hadn't known, such as where his supposed G-spot was located. That, Knox remembered with ballooning horror, explained the acute fascination with the *rosebud*.

His G-spot would remain a virgin, thank you very much.

Edgar had also lectured on attaining the inner orgasm, and had preached against the "squirt," which was reputed to waste a man's sexual energy and rob a woman of her potential multiple orgasms.

In order to avoid the outer orgasm, men were encouraged to practice deep, controlled breathing and to tighten their pubococcygeal and anal sphincter muscles—Knox inwardly shuddered—and to draw the force of their inner ejaculation up through their unblocked chakras, then out of their crown chakra.

Kind of like a volcanic orgasm, Knox had decided after watching Edgar shimmy and shake and look all but ready to blow. Knox winced. Quite frankly, the process looked—and sounded—painful. It had also been very noisy.

Honestly, he hadn't heard so much groaning, moaning and grunting since he'd visited the pig barn at the county fair as a child. Apparently, though, noisy sex promoted tantric energy and so the class was encouraged to sing with their true voices and get as loud as they wished tonight.

Tonight.

Undoubtedly the whole damn villa would come crumbling down around them, brought on by the racket and vibrations of noisy sex.

Edgar and Rupali stood arm and arm in front of the class their cheeks flushed from an exertion Knox would just as soon forget. "This concludes our teachings," Edgar said, smiling. "We hope that what you have learned will promote sexual health and healing, and will deepen your sexual and spiritual connection with your lover."

"Tonight, you will go to your rooms and put all of the lessons we have taught you into practice," Rupali interjected airily. "Open yourselves up and connect with each other as you never have before. Embrace your lover, let your true songs be sung, and seek the harmony of the *kundalini*." She smiled. "There are no additional instructions for tonight. Build upon the intimacies of the shared bath and dinner. Enhance them to fit your purposes, your pleasures. Go…and enjoy. We will meet in the common room and share our experiences and bid our farewells in the morning.'' The class began to disperse eagerly.

Savannah turned to Knox and a tentative, endearing smile curved her lips. ''Well,'' she said nervously.

Anticipation and some other curious emotion not readily identified mushroomed inside him. With effort, he swallowed and threaded his fingers through hers and tugged her toward their room. He grinned. ''Come on, Barbie.''

The walk back to their room seemed to take forever and in those few interminable minutes, a fist of anxiety tightened in Knox's chest, momentarily dousing the perpetual fire he'd carried in his loins.

He'd made love to women countless times, had committed carnal acts so depraved and hedonistic they would make even the unflappable Dr. Ruth blush. Knox was no stranger to sex and was confident in his ability to pleasure a woman.

But Savannah Reeves wasn't just any woman and the importance of that fact had hit him just seconds ago when she'd turned to him with eyes that were equally lit with desire and trepidation. Knox inexplicably knew that this woman—this time with this woman—was going to be different…and it scared the living hell out of him.

He could feel the tension vibrating off her slim frame as well, and wondered if she had suddenly had second thoughts. Knox opened the door and let her pass. Her anxious expression made him feel like a class-A bastard. He'd pushed her into this, he knew. He hadn't left well enough alone and now—

Savannah whirled around as soon as the door closed behind them, grabbed on to the front of his *kurta* and launched herself at his mouth.

Knox staggered back against the wall as the force of her desire blindsided him. Savannah's tongue plunged hungrily in and out of his mouth, suckled him, and burned through any doubts as to why she'd been anxious.

She wanted him.

She was here in his arms, feeding at his mouth, her hands roaming greedily over him, as though she couldn't—wouldn't—ever get enough of him.

Knox sucked in a harsh breath and a strange quiver rippled through his belly. The nudge commenced with an insistent jab. Lust detonated low in his loins, made him want to roar with desire, haul her to the bed and plow into that hot, wet valley between her thighs.

With a growl of pleasure, Knox molded her slim, supple body more closely to his, felt her squirm against him in an unspoken plea for release. Her pebbled breasts raked across his chest, igniting a trail of indescribably perfect sensation.

Savannah drew back. Blue flames danced in her somnolent gaze. "Do you know how I got through that last class?" she asked huskily.

Knox shook his head.

"I kept thinking about getting to do all those

things to you. My hands on your body, you in my mouth…'' She pulled in a breath. "I have a very keen imagination and for the past several hours, I've been imagining this night," she said, her foggy tones almost hypnotic. "Imagining everything that I want to do to you—and with you—and everything I want you to do to me." She cocked her head invitingly toward the bathroom. "Now I want to show you. Whaddya say we start with a bath?"

Savannah stepped back and, in a gesture so inherently sexy it stole his breath, she pulled the *kurta* up over her head and let it drop to the floor. Then, with a saucy wink, she turned and walked to the bathroom.

She'd undoubtedly be the death of him, Knox thought, if indeed a man could expire from sexual stimulation. But, oh, what a way to go…

SAVANNAH POURED a bottle of scented oil that had magically appeared in their bathroom today into the steaming tub and felt a feline smile of satisfaction curl her lips. She'd been waiting for this day forever, had been waiting for this time with him forever, and now—at long last—she would have him.

Repeatedly, she hoped.

Something, warm, hot and languid snaked through her body at the thought, sending a pulse of sensation straight to her quivering womb. Her breasts grew heavy and her nipples tightened and tingled hungrily in anticipation of Knox's hot mouth.

The object of her lusty thoughts chose that moment to stroll naked into the bathroom. Savannah let her gaze roam over his magnificent body slowly, committing to memory each perfect inch of his impressive form. His eyes were dark and slumberous, and burned with a heat she recognized because it sizzled in her as well.

Her gaze skimmed the broad, muscled shoulders, washboard abdomen, lean waist and then settled drunkenly on his fully erect—*enormous*—penis, the one she simply couldn't wait to take into her mouth and, later, feel throbbing deeply inside her. His thighs were powerfully muscled, yet lean and athletic. And, oh, that ass... There was absolutely nothing about him physically that could be improved upon. Even his feet were perfect.

Savannah pulled in a shuddering breath as every cell in her body became hammeringly aware of him, clamoring for him and the cataclysmic release she knew she would find in his arms.

While she'd been openly appraising him, she in turn had been undergoing a similarly intense study. Knox's hot gaze had raked down her body in a leisurely fashion that felt more like a caress than a mere look, and the heat that presently funneled in her womb as a result of that narrow scrutiny was rapidly whipping her insides into a froth of insatiable need.

His lips quirked into a slow sexy grin. "You've told me what you've been thinking about today. Why don't you get in that tub and I'll *show* you what I've been thinking about.''

Oh, sweet heaven. Savannah's bones all but melted. She stepped into the warm, scented water and sank down until only the tips of her breasts peeked above the foggy surface.

Knox slid in behind her so that she sat in the open vee of his thighs. Savannah's eyes fluttered shut and a sound of pure contentment puffed past her smiling lips as he snaked an arm around her waist and tugged her back against him. His warmth engulfed her, the hot, hard length of him pressed against the small of her back. Knox reached around her, filled his cupped hands with water and then palmed her breasts, kneaded them, rolled her beaded nipples between his thumb and forefinger. Savannah gasped, curled her toes and pressed her back more firmly against him.

He nuzzled her neck. ''This was one of the things I've been thinking about,'' Knox murmured huskily. ''Feeling your plump breasts in my hands, thumbing your pouty nipples. Do you have any idea how perfect you are? How absolutely beautiful?'' His hands mimicked his words and played languidly at her sensitized breasts, forcing another gasp of pleasure from her lips.

Savannah didn't bother to answer, but raised an arm, cupped the back of his head and turned to find his lips. She kissed him long and hard, soft and deep, slow yet purposefully, and all the while, Knox continued a magnificent assault on her aching breasts.

Then he moved lower, over her trembling belly, until finally he parted her curls and swept a finger over her throbbing, woefully neglected clit. Savannah jerked as sensation bolted through her, and she whimpered against his plundering mouth.

Knox drew back and slid his fingers into the hot, wet folds of her sex. "I've been wanting to do that as well," he said, rhythmically stroking her. "Feel the slick heat of your body, swallow your gasps, taste your groans."

Savannah's feminine muscles clenched beneath the exquisite pressure of his fingers. A long, slow drag, a swirl over her nub, and back again, over and over with his tender, mind-numbing assault. Her breath came in rapid, helpless puffs. Savannah felt her womb quicken, recognized the sharp tug of the beginning of a climax. She bit her bottom lip, a pathetic attempt to stem the steady flow of longing hurtling through her. He rocked gently behind her, mimicking the steady thought-shattering pressure. It built and built, like the tightening of a screw until something inside her finally—blessedly—snapped. Her body bowed from the shock, the explosion of sensation, and wept with the pulsing torrent and sweet rain of release.

Knox continued to gently rub her, light delicate strokes that made the orgasm seem to go on forever, more than she could bear.

She twisted away from those wicked fingers and turned around, straddled him and kissed him deeply once more. She sucked his tongue, nipped at his lips. The feel of his wet, hard body, slickened with the vaguest hint of oil, felt excessively hedonistic beneath her questing palms. Savannah pulled in a shaky breath as she felt the incredibly long length of him slide along her nether lips. She pressed her aching breasts to his chest and quivered with delight as his masculine hair abraded her sensitive nipples. She slid her hands down the smooth planes of his chest, ran her nails over the hardened nubs of his nipples and was rewarded when Knox hissed with pleasure.

"Damn," he groaned.

Savannah smiled evilly. "Oh, no baby, that's not a damn. *This* merits a damn." She reached down between their practically joined bodies and took him in her hand.

Knox drew in a sharp breath and jerked against her palm. "Y-you're right," he stuttered. "That is most definitely a damn."

Savannah ran her hand up and down the length of him, palmed the sensitive head of his penis and marveled once again over the sheer size of him. He was extraordinarily large, marvelously huge…and for the time being, all hers. Every splendid inch of him.

She worked the length of him, up and down, long steady strokes, feathery touches, but soon touching him simply wasn't enough.

She wanted to taste him.

She gestured toward the steps and gently moved his body in that direction, and eventually managed to put him exactly where she wanted him—in her mouth.

Knox's swiftly indrawn breath was music to her ears. Sing your true songs, indeed, Savannah thought with a smile as she licked the swollen head of his penis. She alternated nibbles and sucks down the sides of him, ran her lips up and down his long length, and cuddled his testicles. Emboldened, she touched her tongue to those, too, and pulled one into her mouth and rolled it around her tongue.

Knox jerked and hissed another tortured breath. "Damn."

Savannah paused her ministrations. "Yeah, that should qualify as a damn." She smiled against him. "And so should this."

With that enigmatic comment, Savannah wrapped her lips around him, took him fully into her mouth and sucked hard. She curled her tongue around him, licked and suckled, over and over, and dragged him deeper and deeper into her mouth. She worked his base, gently massaged his testicles, and slid him in and out of her mouth. Knox's breath grew ragged and his thighs tensed, heralding the arrival of his impending climax.

When the first taste of his salty essence hit her tongue, Savannah drew back, took him in her hand and pumped him hard. She felt the rush of his orgasm shoot through the length of him like a bullet down the barrel of a gun, then felt him jerk and shudder as the hot blast burst from his loins. She milked him, drawing every last ounce of pleasure from him that she could.

Knox halted her ministrations with the touch of his trembling hand. "Enough," he growled. He stood and drew her up with him. "Let's go to bed."

She'd thought he'd never ask, Savannah thought. Knox snagged a towel from the bar and gently swabbed down her body, then hastily ran it over himself as well. Within seconds, they were rolling around the bed, a tangle of desperate arms and legs. The first orgasm had merely taken the edge off, but hadn't begun to dull the attraction. She still wanted him more than she wanted her next breath. Still couldn't wait to feel him plunging into her, couldn't wait to have his hot hands anchored at her waist while she sank down upon him.

Breathing hard, Knox pinned her down and his gaze tangled with hers. "You've tasted me—now I want you to lie still and take it while I taste you."

What? Savannah thought. Did he expect her to argue? She giggled. "Go ahead," she told him. "Eat me."

His eyes widened, then narrowed and his slow, sexy grin melted into one of the most sensual smiles she'd ever seen. "Oh, you are evil."

Savannah raked her nails over his chest. "Yeah...but you like it."

Those dark green eyes twinkled. "Yeah, I do." He bent down and drew her budded nipple into his mouth, pulling the air from her lungs in the process. "And I like this, too."

"Mmm," Savannah sighed. "So do I."

Knox thumbed one tingling nipple while he tortured the other with his mouth. He swiveled his tongue around the sensitive peak, then sucked it deeply into his mouth. Savannah pressed her legs together as the one sensation sparked another deep in her womb. Her clit pulsed and her feminine muscles contracted, begging—crying—for release. Seemingly reading her mind, Knox slid his hand down her shuddering belly and slipped his fingers into her drenched curls.

Savannah whimpered and pressed herself shamelessly against him, willing him to put her out of her sexually frustrated misery. She was on fire, burning up from the inside out, and the only antidote to this mad fever was a shot of him planted deep inside of her.

Knox kissed his way down her belly, swirled his tongue around and inside her navel, and then continued a determined path down to her sex. He knelt between her legs, parted her nether lips, then fastened his mouth onto the small hardened nub of desire hidden in those quivering folds and sucked hard. He worked his tongue up and down her valley, thrust it inside her, then suckled her again. Savannah bowed off the sheet, bucking beneath the most intimate kiss. Lust licked at her veins, and a deep tremble shook her seemingly boneless body.

He slid a finger deep inside her and hooked it around, savoring the moment that she practically arched off the bed. A groan tore from her throat and her eyes all but rolled back into her head.

The ultrasensitive patch of cells could only be her G-spot. Up until this very minute, Savannah hadn't known that she had one.

"Did you…learn that…this weekend?" Savannah asked brokenly as her hands fisted in the sheets.

Knox massaged the tender spot, while lapping at her clit with his wicked tongue. "I improved my technique, yes."

If he improved it any more, she'd undoubtedly burst into flames, shatter and fly into a million little pieces. The thought had no sooner flitted through her mind than the climax caught her completely unaware and broke over her like a high tide, sweeping her under, drowning her in the undertow of sparkling release.

She'd barely caught her breath before Knox snagged a condom from the nightstand, ripped into the package with his teeth, withdrew the thin contraceptive and then swiftly rolled it into place. Seconds later, he'd positioned himself between her thighs and then, with a primal groan of satisfaction, plunged into her.

The room shrank, swelled and then righted itself in the same instant. It was all Savannah could do to keep from passing out, he filled her so very completely. She stilled, waiting for her almost virgin-again body to accommodate his massive size.

"Are you all right?" Knox asked. Concern lined his brow.

Savannah resumed breathing and then tentatively rocked her hips against him, drawing him deeper into her body. "Yes, I am. I just—"

"I just nearly killed you because I plowed into you like a battering ram." He winced. "I'm sorry, I—"

"Knox," Savannah interrupted, "no one appreciates the fact that you have learned to apologize more than me...but we really need to work on your timing."

His face blanked. "My timing?"

"Yes, timing. For instance, now—while you're inside me, where I have wanted you to be for oh-so-long—is not the time to be apologizing. Now you need to be fu—"

The rest of her sentence died a quick death as Knox drew back and plunged into her once more. Savannah hiked her legs up and anchored them around Knox's waist, parlayed his every thrust. She rocked against him, clamped her feminine muscles around the hot, slippery length of him and shuddered with satisfaction as the friction between their joined bodies created a delicious draw and drag as he pumped frantically in and out of her.

Knox bent down and latched his mouth onto one of her nipples, sending another bolt of pleasure down into her quivering loins. Savannah ran her hands down his back, reveling in the taut muscles rippling beneath her palms, the slim hollow of his spine, and then she grabbed his magnificent ass and, with a tormented cry, urged him on. Knox understood her unspoken plea and upped the tempo, pumped harder and faster, pistoned in and out of her.

Harder, faster, and harder still.

She caught another bright flash of release and felt her body freeze with anticipation. Her heart threatened to beat right out of her chest and her breathing came in short, little jagged puffs. The tension escalated, steadily climbing like a Roman candle shot into the sky, then having gone as high as it could, exploded into a billion multicolored stars. Slowly, she drifted back to earth, spent but sated...and thoroughly pleasured.

With a guttural cry of satisfaction, Knox plunged into her one final time, his body bowed with the redeeming rapture of release. He shuddered violently, then his breath left him in one long whoosh and he sagged against her.

Knox rolled them quickly onto his side and fitted her more closely to him. He pressed a lingering kiss in her hair between rapid breaths. "Savannah, that was—I've never—"

Savannah felt a slow smile move across her lips and something warm and tingly bubbled through her chest. "A wordsmith, and yet you're speechless," Savannah teased.

"That," he said meaningfully, "was indescribable."

Savannah heaved a contented sigh. "It really was, wasn't it?"

Knox absently drew circles on her arm. "It was," he agreed.

She'd known it would be, Savannah thought. She'd never doubted it. She'd wanted Knox Webber since the very first moment she'd seen him. She'd yearned for him in secret silence and had nearly gone crazy as a result of the one-sided attraction. Her breathing had barely returned to normal and yet just feeling him next to her did something to her insides. She should be exhausted, she shouldn't be thinking about the delicious weight of his body pressed against hers, or the long, semiaroused length of him nuzzled against her hip.

Yet she was.

Were he to roll over and kiss her right now, she'd eagerly spread her legs and beg him to fill her up once again. The moment Knox had entered her, it was as though a wellspring of repressed emotion had been plumbed. Colors seemed brighter, scents stronger, her entire world had come into sharper focus. In that instant, Rupali's sage words had come back to her. *I don't think your problem lies in the lower chakras...*

And the older woman had been right. Knox had touched her heart. He'd fixed something this weekend that had been broken inside her. If nothing ever came of their time together, then at least she would have that.

Savannah had never felt anything like this before, had never had a lump in her throat after hours of mind-boggling, body-drenching, sweaty, wonderful sex.

But she did right now, and Savannah grimly suspected that were she to truly consider its origin, she would weep with regret.

So she wouldn't.

She'd simply tell herself that the reason she was so utterly moved by their lovemaking was the result of years of pent-up emotion and stress. She'd tell herself that the feelings that were currently taking root in her foolish heart were a product of a weekend of tremendous sexual stimulation, even possibly the result of the tantric rituals. She would tell herself these things…and pray that by the end of this weekend she'd believe them.

The alternative was unacceptable—she wouldn't permit herself to fall in love with Knox Webber…if it wasn't already too late.

13

When Knox awoke on Monday morning, the first few tendrils of pink were spreading across the horizon, chasing away the early gray of dawn. Savannah was spooned with her back to his belly and he'd cupped her breast and slung a thigh over her inert form sometime during the night.

Feeling her next to him, having that delectable body snuggled up against his, engendered a host of sensations, of feelings. Before he'd so much as opened his eyes a smile had unaccountably curled his lips and a light, warm emotion had filled his chest, then inexplicably crowded into his heart.

Knox knew his heart had absolutely no business getting involved in what had happened between him and Savannah—it was supposed to have been sex and nothing more—but he gloomily suspected this feeling currently lurking in his chest was more than he'd bargained for, and definitely more than she had.

Knox had thought that the nudge of the story had brought him here, but he knew better now. The insistent nudge that had propelled him to this place didn't have anything to do with a story...and never had, Knox realized belatedly.

It had been Savannah.

When he'd failed to act on his own, his nudge had taken over and done the business for him, had made sure that he'd found her.

Knox recognized a good thing when he had it, and Savannah Reeves was a good thing. She was bright and witty and charming, and sexy as hell, and just being with her made him feel like a better man, made him *want* to be a better man. Knox didn't have a clue what the future might bring, but the idea of a future without her in it held absolutely no appeal.

He supposed he was in love with her, and he waited for the mental admission to jump-start a wave of panic, for the fist of anxiety to punch him in the gut, at the very least prod his insides with a finger of dread.

It didn't.

Instead, his chest swelled with the sweet, foreign emotion, forcing a contented grunt from his lips. He didn't have any idea how Savannah felt about him and wouldn't allow himself to think about it. If she hadn't fallen in love with him, he'd make her. It was as simple as that.

Given her history, Knox knew he'd have his work cut out for him—she'd have to trust him before she'd love him, he knew—but he hadn't gotten this far in life without patience and tenacity. He had the attraction working in his favor and would just build on that until she was ready for more. As far as a plan went, it might not be the best one, but it was the only one he had at present.

Failure was not an option. Come hell or high water, he'd make Savannah Reeves his.

A glimpse of white at the window snagged his attention. Rupali and Edgar were just scant feet outside their bedroom window. Edgar drew up short and parked a wheelbarrow filled with various shrubs and flowering plants. They were landscaping? Knox wondered. At this hour of the morning? The thought drew a reluctant smile. They were truly a bizarre pair, but this life they'd chosen seemed to fit them.

In fact, tantric sex seemed to fit them, too.

Knox was certain now that the Sheas believed and put into practice everything they taught. They weren't the crooks he'd originally thought them to be. True, some of the practices and beliefs were out of the realm of his comprehension, his scope of understanding, and he seriously doubted he'd ever become a true tantrist, but he no longer believed that it lay out of the realm of possibility—just his.

Knox watched as the Sheas joined hands, lifted their faces to the sky and chanted. An early morning breeze lifted Rupali's long white hair, billowed their *kurtas* out around them. After a moment, they stepped back and Knox watched Rupali draw something from her pocket—multicolored rocks, they seemed to be—and then toss them into the air. To Knox's astonishment, Edgar began to unload the wheelbarrow and place the plants and shrubs where the rocks had fallen.

That explained the whimsical feel to the landscaping he'd noticed when they'd first gotten here, Knox thought with soft, disbelieving amusement.

Savannah stirred beside him and he bent his head and pressed a kiss to her achingly smooth cheek. A lump of emotion formed in his throat, and for one terrifying instant, Knox's considerable confidence wavered and he wondered if he'd really be able to make her love him. Could he really do it?

A sleepy smile curled her lips and she stretched languidly beside him. "Good morning," she murmured groggily.

Knox's gaze caressed her face, lingered over each and every line and curve. "So far," he said. "I'm here with you."

Savannah sighed with sleepy pleasure and rolled to burrow into his chest. She nuzzled his neck and snaked an arm around his waist. The hard-on he'd awoken with promptly jerked for sport. But that was hardly surprising, was it? He was a man and, were that not enough explanation, he was a man in bed with a naked woman.

"What time is it?" she asked.

"It's early. Pushing six, I'd say."

She smoothed her hand up his side, sending a wave of gooseflesh skittering across his skin. Smiling, Knox sucked in a trembling breath.

"Good," she murmured. "We've got time."

"Time for what?"

"Here, I'll show you."

Savannah rolled him onto his back and straddled him. Her wet sex rode the ridge of his erection and Knox watched her eyes flutter shut and her lips slip into one of the most sensual smiles he'd ever seen. With a growl of satisfaction, he anchored his hands on the sweet swell of her hips and rocked her against him.

The picture she made in that moment was utterly incredible. Those jet-black bed-head curls sprouted in sexy disarray all over her head and the rosy tint of sleep clung to her creamy cheeks. Her eyes were lit with the blue flame of desire, still slumberous and heavy lidded, weighted with the vestiges of sleep. Pale pink nipples crowned the full globes of her breasts, and her belly was gently rounded and completely feminine. The thatch of silky curls at the apex of her thighs rocked against him and...

And the rest of that thought fragmented as Savannah took him in her hand, swiftly sheathed him with a condom, then slowly sank down onto him. Her wet, tight heat gloved him so thoroughly that it ripped the very breath from his lungs.

Savannah's eyes fluttered shut. She smiled with sublime satisfaction and bit her bottom lip. A purr emanated from her throat as she buried his dick as far into her heat as she possibly could.

She flexed her naughty muscles around him. "Do you have any idea how long I've been wanting to do this? How many times I've done it in my dreams?'' she asked. She lifted her hips and settled onto him once more.

''N-no,'' Knox breathed raggedly. ''Tell me.''

Savannah winced with pleasure, slid up and down in a long, sinuous motion. He felt the greedy clench and release of her body as she moved above him, felt the exquisite friction of their joined parts.

''More times…than I…can conceivably count… this weekend.'' Her breath came in startled little puffs as she upped the tempo, rode him harder.

''I would have g-gladly accommodated you,'' Knox replied, thrusting into her, matching his rhythm to hers. Savannah's skin glistened, had flushed into a becoming rosy hue. She arched her neck and little nonsensical sounds—the sound of great sex—bubbled up from her throat.

The fire in his loins rapidly became an inferno that engulfed every inch of him. He felt her tense, watched her mouth open in a silent gasp. She pumped harder and harder on top of him, rode him frantically, clearly racing for the brass ring of release. Knox leaned up, latched his mouth around one nipple and sucked hard, flattening the crown of her breast deep into his mouth. He reached down between their joined bodies and massaged the nub hidden in the wet folds of her sex.

Savannah cried out, bit her lip and whimpered.

He felt her muscles contract, felt her entire body still in awe of the explosion of the coming climax.

The gentle pulsing and rush of heat was all it took to send Knox past the point of endurance and he joined her there in the brilliant flash of release.

Savannah sagged against his chest, not pulling away, but keeping him inside her. Something about the gesture made him want to roar his approval, made him feel more elementally manly. Instead, he trailed his trembling fingers down her spine, then slid his hands back up and hugged her close.

Savannah leaned up and glanced at the top of his head. Her brow creased with perplexity.

Knox frowned. "What? Is something wrong with my hair, because if it is," he said, imitating her, "this is as good as it gets and—"

He felt her laugh against him. "No, it's not your hair. I was just looking for some lotus blossoms. I know this is going to come as a shock…but I can't find any."

Knox chuckled. "Come as a shock, eh? I didn't feel any lotus blossoms fly out of my skull, but I sure thought my head was going to blow off during that last go-around." He lowered his voice. "That was awesome."

She flushed adorably. "Thank you. I try."

"Ah, so I'm not the only one who has learned how to take a compliment."

Her twinkling gaze met his and she winced with regret. "I hate to, but we've got to get up."

"I know," Knox said reluctantly.

"Everyone will be giving their progress reports

this morning. It'll be interesting to see what everyone will have to say.''

He'd thought about that as well. He arched a brow and lazily swirled circles on her back. ''Given any thought as to what you're going to say?'' he asked innocently.

Savannah gently raised herself off him and rolled back onto her side of the bed. He immediately missed her warmth. ''Yes, as a matter of fact I have.''

Knox waited. ''Well?'' he finally prompted.

She swiveled her head to look at him. ''I'm going to say that my 'sacred space' has never been so magnificently illuminated, and that you have the biggest 'wand of light' I've ever seen.''

His ''wand of light'' stirred at the compliment. ''High praise, indeed.''

''What about you? Surely you're going to correct my frigid-unable-to-climax legacy.''

Knox grinned. ''You can bet your sweet ass, baby. I'm going to report a multiple orgasm breakthrough and sing the praises of your 'sacred space.'''

She nodded, seemingly pleased. ''Ugh,'' she groaned. ''We've got to get up. They'll be starting soon, and we really need to hear everyone's input for the story.'' She paused. ''When are we going to work on this story, by the way?''

''I thought we could work on it on the way back. Is that all right with you?''

Savannah inclined her head. ''Sure, that'll be fine. Think we'll have time to finish it?''

"Yeah. I could be wrong, but I think this is going to be one of those stories that tells itself. If not, we can always finish it at my place...or yours."

She stilled and something in her gaze brightened and dimmed all in the same instant. What? Knox thought. Did she think that this had simply been a weekend fling? If so, he needed to swiftly disabuse her of that notion. She also needed to understand that he wasn't the bastard who'd broken her heart—he was someone she could trust.

"I'd, uh, planned on you spending quite a bit of time from here on out at my place, and hoped that I'd be invited to yours," Knox said, laying it all out on the line. He didn't want to frighten her, nor did he intend to mislead her.

It was a short story. He wanted her. The end.

When she didn't readily reply, Knox felt the first prickle of unease move through his belly. Savannah just stood there, looking at him with an unreadable expression that made his insides knot with anxiety. "Have I read too much into this?" he asked.

"No," she replied hesitantly, and his tension lessened slightly. "I, uh..." She shrugged helplessly. "To be honest, I hadn't let myself think beyond this weekend. I didn't want to get my ho— I just thought it would be best to hedge my bets."

"And now?" he prodded.

"And now my thoughts are along the same lines as yours."

"So we'll be spending a lot of time together,

then?'' he queried lightly, just to be sure they were on the same page.

He caught the feline smile that curved her lips a fraction of a second before she turned and headed toward the bathroom. ''You can bet your sweet ass,'' she said, giving him a wonderful view of hers.

SAVANNAH DIDN'T KNOW what to make of Knox's morning-after behavior. Frankly, she'd expected him to be charming but withdrawn. She'd expected him to try and put a more professional spin on their relationship, to try to regain some lost ground. In short, she'd expected him to act like a typical man…but as she'd learned over the course of this weekend, Knox Webber wasn't a typical man.

He'd done the one and only thing Savannah *hadn't* expected—he'd expressed a wish to see her again and, though she was trying very hard not to let her heart get carried away, if she'd understood him correctly—and she thought she had—he wanted to see her *a lot*.

Considering she'd fallen head over heels in love with him this weekend, Savannah decided that was very promising.

There had been several times over the course of last night and this morning when she'd caught Knox giving her poignantly tender looks, but Savannah had convinced herself they'd been wishful thinking, the product of her imagination…anything but what they were. She'd been so careful of getting her hopes up

that she'd ignored every sign of some deeper emotion—and there had been plenty, now that she
thought about it. Belated delight bloomed in her
chest.

She'd have to be careful, of course. Tread carefully—she'd been burned too many times not to be
a little reticent. But the idea that she might have
found someone who genuinely wanted her—after almost a lifetime of being alone—was so achingly
sweet.

The back of her throat burned with emotion and
her insides quivered with hesitant joy. She'd longed
to be wanted, to be part of a family for what seemed
like forever. Someone to spend Thanksgiving and
Christmas with, to help celebrate her birthday. Little
things that other people simply took for granted were
things that Savannah had, for the most part, never
had.

Savannah didn't know anything about the Webber
family other than that they were wealthy and that
they didn't approve of Knox's career. Did that mean
they wouldn't approve of her either? Savannah wondered, remembering Gib's family with a shudder.
More important, would it matter to Knox if they
didn't? Savannah paused consideringly, mulling the
question over. She honestly didn't think so. If he'd
gone ahead and chosen to be a journalist despite their
protests, then surely he'd use the same headstrong
logic when choosing a wife.

Wife?

Jeez, where had that thought come from? Savannah shot a surreptitious glance at Knox to make sure that the absurd thought hadn't somehow been transmitted from her brow chakra to his via mental telepathy. Presently, Knox was working the room, subtly interrogating couples about their tantric experience. She should be doing the same thing, Savannah thought with a stab of self-disgust, instead of mooning over her new boyfriend.

Still her shoulders drooped with relief and her heart inexplicably swelled when his gaze caught hers. Those dark green orbs shone with humor and a hint of kindled lust, but thankfully no panic or fear, which she definitely would have detected should he have been privy to her *wife* thought.

So much for treading carefully, Savannah thought with a rueful smile. She absently twisted the thin gold band on her finger, and a prick of regret pierced her heart. She knew it was foolish, but she didn't want to give it back. She wanted to keep it and wear it and be everything to Knox that the token implied.

Knox sidled up next to her and nuzzled her ear. "Is it getting on your nerves?"

Savannah started guiltily. "What?"

"The ring. Is it getting on your nerves?"

She swallowed and forced a smile. "No, not at all. I was just admiring it. Don't let me forget to give it back to you. Maybe you can take them back and your jeweler will give you a refund."

"And risk bad karma?" Knox asked playfully. He

shook his head. "I think I'll keep them. You never know when you might need a set of bands."

With that enigmatic comment, Knox steered her toward the front of the room where the Sheas waited to bid their farewells. "Good morning, class." Edgar beamed. "Rupali and I have had the opportunity to speak with several of you this morning and, by all accounts, last night was a resounding success."

Rupali smiled serenely. "We are so very thrilled for each and every one of you. Our time together has come to an end, but please continue to use what you have learned here in your daily lives. Take the love and harmony you've found in our house home to yours. Remember truth and healing, sing your true songs, speak with your true voices and draw from the energy of Mother Earth. Cleanse your chakras, forbid blocks and continue to grow in spiritual and sexual health. Women, honor your man, never cease longing to please him. He will return your effort with pleasure tenfold."

"Likewise, men, honor your woman. Respect her, be worthy of her love, and strive to continually bring her more pleasure. For to do these things for another is to do them for yourself."

Edgar and Rupali joined hands. "We bid you well," they said in unison.

Knox threaded Savannah's fingers through hers and squeezed. "Well, that's that then. You ready?"

Savannah nodded. She supposed so. They'd donned their regular clothes this morning for the journey home, and already the bra and undies seemed to chafe her skin. She never thought she'd say it but, like Knox, she'd grown rather fond of the free feeling of the *kurta*.

Knox had gone out this morning and loaded the car, so everything had been packed. There was absolutely no reason to linger, and yet, for some reason, Savannah found herself curiously reluctant to leave.

"Barbie," Rupali called. "May I have a word before you go, please?"

Savannah nodded. Knox gave her a perplexed look, but left at her prodding when she promised to meet him at the car.

Savannah cleared her throat. "You wanted to speak with me?" she asked nervously. Something about this woman's perceptive gaze unnerved her.

Rupali laid a soft, bejeweled hand on her arm. "Did you experience any breakthroughs this weekend? Did your world shift and come back into brighter focus?"

Unbidden tears stung her eyes. A short laugh erupted from her throat and she nodded. "Yes," Savannah choked out. "It did."

Rupali nodded in understanding. "Good. I'd hoped you would. My third eye is my strongest chakra, and I had a feeling about you," she told her. "I know that you'll have cause to doubt, but you'll be all right now, you know."

"Thank you," Savannah said, inexplicably reassured by this woman's calm assessment.

To her surprise, Rupali leaned forward and hugged her in a motherly fashion, a gesture Savannah hadn't had in such a long, long time. She blinked back tears once more. "Go, child," Rupali told her. "He's waiting."

Savannah withdrew from Rupali's embrace and hurried out to the car. Knox took one look at her and his jaw went hard. "What happened?" he demanded. "What's wrong?"

"Nothing," Savannah said shakily, wiping the moisture from beneath her eyes. "Just women stuff. It's nothing. Really."

Knox didn't look convinced. "You're sure you're all right? You're sure there's nothing wrong?"

His concern touched her deeply, made her want to vault across the seat, plant herself in his lap, and rain kisses all over his outraged face. A champion, what a novel experience. Savannah's heart galloped in her chest and joy fizzed through her, until finally it bubbled right out of her mouth in a stream of delighted laughter.

Knox looked at her askance. Worry replaced the outrage. "Are you sure you're all right?"

"Yes," Savannah said emphatically. For the first time in her life *everything* felt all right.

14

ON ANY GIVEN DAY, Knox typically enjoyed walking into the offices of the *Chicago Phoenix*. His world. He loved the hustle and bustle, the murmur of conversation and the ceaseless ring of the telephones. This was the chaotic world of the newsroom, where breaking news mingled with the mundane, juicy gossip and the occasional super-hot exposé.

Their tantric sex piece wouldn't be considered any of those things, Knox knew, and yet it had turned out to be a great story that both he and Savannah were very proud of. The article had come together so seamlessly that it had, as predicted, practically written itself. He and Savannah had simply framed it up with words, ones that he hoped would do justice to their experience with the ancient technique. The piece had been informative, skeptical in a humorous way, yet left plenty of room for possibility. Ultimately it had let readers draw their own conclusions.

Knox had always worked alone, had always considered writing a solitary business. But, to his delight, he and Savannah had worked extremely well together. Their styles complemented each other and they intuitively played to each other's weaknesses. In short, they were great together. They wrote like they made love—splendidly.

Knox had left Savannah at her apartment eight hours ago and, during that time, he hadn't stopped thinking about her.

He simply couldn't.

She consumed his every waking thought and had even invaded his dreams. And he wanted to know her every thought, her every dream, her every secret. He wanted to learn all of her little idiosyncrasies, to wake up with her in the morning and go to bed with her each night. He wanted to shower her with the affection she'd missed as a child, to make up for every heartache she'd ever experienced. He wanted her to trust him…and he wanted to be her hero.

Basically, he just *wanted* her.

Knox felt the perpetual smile he'd worn since yesterday morning when his whole world had changed. To his surprise, he found himself whistling as he strolled into work this morning.

It had been late when they'd arrived back in Chicago, so after dropping Savannah off at her apartment, Knox had brought the piece down here to leave for Chapman to proofread. His boss usually arrived a good hour before the rest of the staff, and Knox knew that Chapman would be eager to read the article. Knox was equally eager to hear what Chapman thought of it.

A look through the glass confirmed his boss was

in. Knox rapped on the door and Chapman beckoned him inside.

"It's brilliant," Chapman said. "It's damn brilliant. I read it first thing this morning."

Knox slowly released the pent-up breath he'd been holding. "Thank you, sir. We're proud of it."

"And I have a surprise for you—it'll run with your byline only."

Something cold slithered through him. Knox blinked, certain he'd misunderstood. "Come again?"

"You're not sharing your byline. I never intended for you to. Ms. Reeves needed to be taught a lesson, Webber, and this is the way I've planned to do it."

Fury whipped through Knox. "Look, I don't know what's going on—"

"And you don't need to, as it doesn't concern you."

"Doesn't concern me?" Knox repeated hotly. "Like hell. I just spent the entire weekend working with her. *We*—not I—just wrote a great piece." Knox glared at him. "She did the work, she deserves the credit."

Chapman smiled infuriatingly. "Be that as it may, she's not going to get it."

Knox fisted his hands at his sides and silently willed himself to calm down. Beating the hell out of his boss, which was exceedingly tempting at the moment, wouldn't benefit anyone.

He'd heard stories about Chapman's legendary ruthlessness—hell, everyone in this city had—but had always thought they'd been exaggerated. While he'd never considered Chapman a friend, he'd none-theless always respected the man and his opinion. Clearly, that was at an end, Knox thought, swallow-ing his bitter disappointment.

"I don't appreciate being dragged into this," Knox said, his jaw set so hard he feared it would crack. "Furthermore, I don't care for your methods."

"You don't have to." Chapman narrowed his eyes. "Have you forgotten who is the boss here, Webber, whose name is on that door? If so, let me refresh your memory—it's mine. I do things my way, and people who don't realize that—or choose to ig-nore it—pay accordingly or end up unemployed. Have I made myself clear?"

Knox smirked as a red rage settled over his brain. "Perfectly."

With that, Knox pivoted and stormed from Chap-man's office. He knew any argument was pointless. Several co-workers called out greetings, but Knox wasn't in any frame of mind to play the amiable rich boy today. He needed to intercept Savannah before she came in this morning and prepare her for Chap-man's little bomb.

More important, he needed to make sure she un-derstood that he hadn't played any part in it.

Anxiety roiled in his gut and his heart stumbled in his chest as the implications of what had just tran-spired in Chapman's office fully surfaced in Knox's furious mind.

He could lose her because of this.

He could lose her.

He'd forced her hand, had gone to Chapman and had made her go on that assignment when she'd expressly and repeatedly insisted that she didn't want to go. She'd undoubtedly believe that he'd been in on it, that he and Chapman had plotted out her punishment together. Hell, even he had to admit that he looked guilty. What was it he'd told her? *Don't make me play hardball.* Knox snorted and shook his head. What a pompous idiot he'd been.

It wouldn't matter that they'd made love all weekend, that they'd shared the most mind-blowing, soul-shattering sex, that he'd all but told her he'd fallen head over hills in love with her. Granted, he hadn't said those words per se, but surely she'd understood the implication. He hadn't been able to keep his hands off her, for pity's sake.

But none of it would matter, Knox needlessly reminded himself. She didn't trust him with her heart yet and if she talked with Chapman before Knox had a chance to talk to her, he most likely would never get the opportunity.

Nausea curdled in his stomach.

Just what in the hell had she supposedly done that would make Chapman sink to such measures of retribution? Knox wondered angrily. What unforgivable offense had she committed? Knox hadn't heard the first rumor, so whatever it was had been kept quiet.

Secrets didn't typically last in a newsroom, but obviously this one had.

Knox breathed relief when the elevator doors finally opened, hurried inside and impatiently stabbed the button for the lobby. In the end it didn't matter what she had or hadn't done.

The only thing that mattered was making sure that she understood that *he* hadn't had anything to do with this mess—that he hadn't betrayed her, and he would do whatever was necessary to make her believe it.

His insides twisted with dread and he broke out in a cold sweat. He wouldn't lose her, dammit. Knox slammed his fist into the elevator wall.

He couldn't.

SAVANNAH ROCKED back on her heels and waited patiently for the elevator to deliver her to the eleventh floor, home of the *Chicago Phoenix.* She'd awoken this morning with a lighthearted smile and the irrepressible urge to get to work. Savannah knew her anxiousness had less to do with the desire to do her job and more to do with the desire to see—and do, she thought wickedly—Knox.

It had been late by the time they'd gotten back to Chicago and, though he'd all but turned her into a quivering puddle of need with that marathon goodnight kiss, Savannah hadn't asked Knox to spend the night. He'd been very proud of their piece—as had she—and Knox had wanted to swing by the *Phoenix* and leave the article on Chapman's desk so that he could read it first thing this morning.

Though she didn't particularly care for their boss, it was obvious that Knox valued the older man's opinion. Savannah supposed that in absence of his father's approval, Knox had attached special meaning to Chapman's. She had the old bastard's number, though, and knew Knox's trust had been misplaced. She dreaded when Knox would reach that conclusion as well. She'd swallowed more than her share of disappointment and knew that it left a bitter aftertaste.

As for her, Savannah had wanted to get here early this morning to hear Chapman's opinion of the story as well. She hoped that, having gone on this little trip at his bidding to serve penance for her so-called offenses, he would back off now and let her return to her job.

Savannah chuckled. Her punishment had backfired.

Big time.

Chapman had sent her on this trip with the notion of knuckling her under, of humbling her. Little did he know that she and Knox had found something indescribably perfect together, that they'd spent the weekend in hedonistic splendor, and that he'd unwittingly forced her to admit what her heart had known all along—Knox Webber was The One.

Rather than continuing to nurse her animosity toward Chapman, it occurred to Savannah that she should thank him instead.

Doing the tantric piece with Knox had been utterly wonderful. They'd worked amazingly well together and the story had only served to whet her appetite for more. She was tired of covering the mundane, had grown weary of the half-assed assignments Chapman had foisted upon her since she'd pissed him off. With luck, when she walked into the office this morning, things would have finally changed for the better.

Savannah had no more than set foot out of the elevator when Chapman summoned her into his inner sanctum. Suppressing a secret smile, she squared her shoulders and strolled in.

"Good morning, sir," Savannah said.

"Good morning," he returned, his smile a wee bit too smug for Savannah's liking. A finger of trepidation slid down her spine. "I've had a chance to read the article you and Webber did." He inclined his head. "Great stuff."

Savannah's tension eased marginally and she smiled. "I'm glad you like it, sir. Knox and I are very proud of it."

He winced regretfully. "I've only got one minor revision, though."

"Certainly. What's that?"

"The byline," Chapman said, his fat lips curling into a malevolent smile. "I'm eliminating a name from it—yours."

For all intents and purposes, the ground shifted beneath Savannah's feet. Her ears rung, and nausea pushed into her throat. She blinked, astonished. "I'm sorry?"

"I'm sure you are."

"*What?*"

"I never intended to let you take credit for this story. You need to learn some respect, Ms. Reeves. You also need to learn to heed my wishes. From this day forward, you will do that. Do you understand?" he asked in softly ominous tones. "I am the boss here and you will answer my questions when I ask them, regardless of your so-called journalistic integrity...or else. Let this be a lesson to you, my dear. Don't screw with me. You'll lose."

"But I did the work," Savannah said angrily.

He leaned back in his seat and stacked his hands behind his head. "But you won't get credit for it, or any other article until you learn some respect."

The implication of everything she'd just heard hit Savannah like an unexpected blow to the belly. She swallowed her disappointment, her anger—ate it until she thought for sure she would vomit.

A horrible suspicion rose. "But Knox—"

"—has done and will always do exactly what I tell him to," Chapman said meaningfully. His eyes glittered with evil humor. "He's a model staffer."

Savannah crossed her arms over her chest and snorted with bitter regret. Her world dimmed back into its usual muted focus and the light heart she'd enjoyed only moments ago instantly turned to lead.

"I see," she finally managed. She had to push the words from her seared throat.

"Good," Chapman said. "I thought that you would when you'd been shown the bigger picture."

Without further comment, Savannah turned and walked out of Chapman's office, through the busy newsroom, and eventually out of the building. She got into her car and, amazingly dry-eyed, drove across town to her small efficiency apartment.

For those long interminable minutes, she was utterly and completely numb. It had been like Chapman's words had cut off the circulation to her feelings, had prevented her from experiencing even the least amount of emotion.

But the second Savannah entered her apartment, that tourniquet was released and the pain ripped through her, wrenching an anguished, silent sob from her throat. It drove her to the floor, the weight of the torment so unbelievably unbearable.

Savannah knew this woeful routine, had been a player in this all too familiar scene. But she didn't understand now any more than she ever had, just exactly what she'd done to deserve this kind of heartache. What made her so unworthy of even a sliver of happiness? A lump formed in her tight throat. Hot tears slipped down her cheeks and splashed onto her shaking hands. She bit her lip to stem the flow, but it didn't work. The pain was an emotion that had to come out, and this was the body's natural way to cleanse itself of hurts.

He'd known, damn him. He'd had to have known, and Chapman, the vengeful jerk, had all but told her so.

Knox has done and will always do exactly what I tell him...

And obviously he had, Savannah thought miserably as another dagger of regret twisted in her chest. Knox had forced her to take that trip, hadn't he? Had gone to Chapman when she refused. Savannah didn't think that Knox had known why she was going to be punished—he'd seemed genuinely curious about that—but she didn't doubt for a minute that he'd known what was going to happen. He'd known that Chapman never planned to let her have that byline. Had known that all of her effort had been for naught.

And if that weren't a bad enough betrayal, he'd let her go and make a fool out of herself by admitting her damned attraction. Had let her give him her body—and her heart, though he didn't know it. Humiliation burned her cheeks and her heart drooped pitifully in her chest.

Savannah had fancifully imagined spending the rest of her life with him, had imagined them working together, celebrating accomplishments, holidays, all of life's major events. She'd imagined waking up with him and going to bed with him. Had imagined a happily-ever-after.

She pulled in a shaky breath as another tear

scalded her cheek. Clearly it had all been just that—a figment of her lonely imagination.

The whole weekend had been about the story, after all.

KNOX HAD SPENT the entire day and the majority of the night trying to make Savannah listen to him. But she wouldn't. He'd repeatedly knocked on her door. He'd alternately called her cell and her home phone number, had even filled her answering machine tape with the whole sordid explanation. But none of it had done one whit of good, and as the day had progressed, he'd become increasingly panicked and afraid that nothing ever would.

The one and only time she'd answered the phone, it had not been with a customary hello, but a couple of succinct words that, frankly, he couldn't believe she'd said. He'd been so shocked she'd hung up on him before he'd had the time to frame a reply.

Knox was at a loss. He simply didn't know what else to do. He'd tried reasoning with Chapman once more, but to no avail. Chapman held fast to his position and wouldn't relent. The story would run with Knox's byline only, and Knox knew if that happened, he and Savannah would never be able to patch things up. Frankly, even without that in the scenario, he wasn't so confident that he could bridge the chasm between them.

Though he knew that he shouldn't be, a part of him was angry with her for thinking so little of him. How could she possibly believe that he'd known about this? After what they'd shared, what they'd done together, how could she continue to doubt him?

True, evidence certainly existed to the contrary, but he'd honestly thought that after he'd explained everything, his word would have been enough to exonerate him. Knox blew out a frustrated breath. It probably would have been with anyone *but* Savannah. She'd been hurt, disappointed too many times. She didn't trust anyone. He wondered—even if by some miracle they got past this—would she ever fully trust him? Or would she continue to paint him with the same brush of uncertainty she used on everyone else?

To his surprise, Knox found himself back at the office. Aside from the typesetters, only a few diehard employees were there at this hour. Knox stilled as the beginnings of an idea stirred.

Only the typesetters…

When Knox had decided to pursue a career in journalism, he'd made a point of knowing the business from the ground up. He'd had a passion for the process and had wanted to experience it all—from the stories and articles that went into the papers, to layout and design, and finally…typesetting.

The idea gelled, sending a course of adrenaline rushing through his blood.

A slow smile curled his lips. Savannah Reeves would have her byline…and Knox would have her.

SAVANNAH'S HEAD FELT like it had been stuffed with cotton. Her eyes were swollen and her nose would undoubtedly require a skin graft to remove the red. But she was alive and healthy and, if for no other reason than her heart continued to beat, she'd live.

She'd heard of people dying due to grief or a broken heart, but Savannah told herself that she'd been made of sterner stuff, and surely she'd sustained more than this. If it felt like she hadn't, or if she sometimes wandered into a room and forgot what she'd been doing, then she simply told herself that it would pass.

Eventually.

But she would get over it.

Knox had called repeatedly, had knocked on her door, had left so many messages on her machine that after the fifth one, she'd hit the erase button. For one anguished second, she'd almost let herself believe him—he'd sounded so desperately sincere—but then reason had returned and she'd clung to her anger. He and Chapman had made a fool of her once—she'd be damned before she'd let them do it again.

Savannah had called in sick to work—something she'd never done before—and had decided to take this day and pull herself back together. She couldn't afford to quit, as she wasn't independently wealthy like Knox, so faxing her resignation wasn't a viable option—attractive, yes, but simply not prudent. She would, however, take a few minutes to update her résumé and put out a few feelers. As soon as she landed another job, she'd tell them both to kiss off.

A reluctant grin curved Savannah's lips. She'd said worse to Knox last night.

The one and only time she'd finally given in to her frustration, she'd answered the phone and growled a couple of choice words she'd never said before right into his ear. She'd taken advantage of his stunned silence to hang up on him. Savannah had finally grown weary of hearing the phone ring and the answering machine messages, so she'd unplugged them. A brief reprieve, she knew, as she'd have to go back to work tomorrow and deal with the whole sordid business, but for the time being she simply wanted to be left alone.

Her heart squeezed painfully in her chest as she shuffled to the door to get her paper. Might as well take a look at the damned thing, Savannah thought. It had certainly cost her enough.

Coffee in hand, she trudged back to her sofa, sat down and, with trembling fingers, finally unfurled the paper. She found the article on page three under the heading Tantric Sex—Old New Fad Or Stranger Than Fiction? Not a bad title, Savannah thought and was in the middle of a shrug when the byline snagged her attention.

By Savannah Reeves and Knox Webber.

Savannah blinked, astounded. Her heart began to race. But how had that happened? What had changed Chapman's mind? It had been thoroughly set, Savannah knew. In one of the many messages left on her machine, Knox had promised to find a way to fix this, but she hadn't believed him. Had he done this? she wondered, hope sprouting in her traitorous breast. Had Knox somehow managed to change Chapman's mind?

Well, there was only one way to find out. Savannah tossed the paper aside, scrambled from the couch and plugged her phone back in. She hit speed-dial and Chapman answered on the first ring.

"Make it quick," her boss said by way of greeting.

"Sir, this is Savannah Re—"

"I know exactly who this is," he snapped. "What do you want?"

Savannah gritted her teeth and resisted the infantile urge to smash the receiver against the wall. "I wanted to thank you for going ahead and giving me my byline. I really—"

"Don't thank me, Ms. Reeves. I had no intention of giving you that byline. You can thank Webber. He came down here last night and distracted a typesetter and added your name to the article," Chapman said stiffly. "He's been terminated."

Savannah gasped. *"You fired him?"*

"Speedily," Chapman said. "One more misstep and you'll be down at the unemployment office applying for benefits right along with him." The dial tone rang in her ear.

Savannah sank onto the edge of her sofa and let the weight of that conversation sink in before trying to stand again. Knox had distracted a typesetter?

He'd added her name? He'd gotten fired because of it? Savannah massaged her throbbing temples. It was simply too much to take in.

What on earth had possessed him to do such a reckless thing? True, Knox had always been Chapman's golden boy but, regardless of that status, Knox had surely realized Chapman would never tolerate such an overt act of defiance from one of his employees, golden boy or no. Knox had to have known that particular act of insubordination would put him out of a job. He'd had to know…and yet he'd done it.

For her? she wondered hesitantly.

Savannah stilled. She'd assumed many things on Knox's behalf over the past twenty-four hours. Sitting here and making assumptions based on word-of-mouth testimony didn't make good journalistic sense.

She'd need to go to the source.

KNOX HAD BEGUN his morning by getting fired and things had steadily proceeded to worsen from there. his mother had made her weekly you-should-come-to-work-for-your-father spiel and when she'd asked him about things at the paper, he'd made the monumental mistake of telling her he'd been fired. Since then his father had called, his sister, and his brother. Undoubtedly, his entire family—all of which was employed by Webber Investments—would be lobbying for him to join the family business.

It wasn't going to happen. Knox was a writer.

He'd find another job in his field. He would not go to work for his father.

Besides, he'd known last night when he'd made the decision to add her name to the byline that he'd lose his job. Knox grunted. Hell, it had been a no-brainer. But when it had come right down to it, making sure that Savannah knew that he was in this for the long haul, that he hadn't betrayed her and that he was worthy of her trust had been more important.

If this sacrifice wasn't enough, then he'd just think of something else until he finally convinced her that she could depend on him. Where others had failed, he would not. It was as simple as that.

Provided he could ever get her to speak to him again, Knox thought. He'd tried to call her again last night, and then again this morning, to tell her to be sure and get her paper, but apparently she'd unplugged her phone and answering machine because her line had simply rung and rung. Patience and persistence, the bigger picture, Knox told himself as he heaved a hearty sigh and dialed her number once again.

He muttered a curse and disconnected when his doorbell rang. His mother, no doubt, Knox thought with a spurt of irritation as he strode angrily to the door. He didn't have time for this, dammit. He needed to get in touch with Savannah. Needed to try—

Knox drew up short as he swung open his door and found the author of his present heartache standing on his threshold. His greedy gaze roamed over her. Her hair looked as if it had never seen a brush and her pale blue eyes were puffy and swollen. Her nose was red and a mangled tissue poked from the pocket of her wrinkled denim shirt. She looked like hell, but a hell he'd gladly embrace.

Hope bloomed in his chest. "Savannah?"

"I needed to talk to you, and calling seemed too impersonal. Mind if I come in?"

Still stunned, Knox belatedly opened the door. "Uh, sure."

Knox guided her into his living room and gestured for her to sit down.

She gazed around his spacious apartment with an appraising eye. "Nice place."

Knox rubbed the back of his neck. "Thanks."

"I heard a rumor today and I wondered if you could confirm it."

"I'll try. What was it?"

"That you went down to the paper last night, distracted a typesetter and added my name to our story, and that you got fired because of it. Is that true?"

Knox blew out a breath. "Yeah, that about sums it up."

Savannah sprang from the couch and glared at him accusingly. "You idiot! What did you do that for? Didn't you know you'd get fired? Have you lost your mind?" she ranted, that blue gaze flashing fire.

Frankly, this was not how Knox had imagined this scene playing out. He was supposed to be a hero, dammit, not an idiot. She was supposed to be grateful, fall into his arms and profess her undying love.

"No, I haven't lost my mind," he said tightly. "I've lost something a great deal more important than that."

She frowned, looking thoroughly irritated. "What exactly is that?"

"My heart."

She stilled, and her frantic gaze finally rested to meet his. "Y-your heart?"

"That's right. You're here for the facts, aren't you? Well, the fact is this—I fell in love with you this weekend. I didn't know anything about Chapman's plans, and didn't know any other way to convince you of it." Knox shrugged. "So I added your byline...and the rest is history."

"But what about your job?" she asked breathlessly. "You loved your job."

Jeez, he'd just told her that he loved her, and she was still harping about the damned job. When was she going to get it?

"Savannah, I don't give a damn about the job if it means that I'm going to lose you. Your trust means more." Knox stood and traced a heart on her cheek. His gaze searched her tormented one. "*You* mean more. I can get another job, baby. But *you're* irreplaceable."

Knox watched her gaze soften and a smile tremble across her lips. He breathed an inaudible sigh of relief. "So are you," she said. Savannah pulled her cell phone from the pocket of her jeans and punched in a number. "Chapman, Savannah Reeves here. I quit." Then she casually ended the call and, with a cry of delight, launched herself into his arms.

"I'm s-so sorry," she cried brokenly. "I should have known better—I should have listened to you. But I was so afraid of getting hurt, I—I just couldn't." She drew back and looked up at him. Blue mist shimmered in her eyes. "Thank you so much for doing this for me. I just— I don't—"

The feeling of immense dread he'd been carrying around for the past day promptly fled and his chest swelled with sweet, giddy emotion. "I know," Knox said, and cut off her inarticulate attempts to describe the indescribable.

"I, uh, love you, too, you know," Savannah said shyly.

"Yeah, I know." He cupped her cheek in his hand. "But will you ever trust me?"

Something shifted in her gaze and Savannah stepped out of his arms and turned around. Knox panicked. He'd pushed her too far again. He'd asked for too much. Dammit.

"Savannah—"

She fell backward and right into his suddenly outstretched arms. The blind-trust test. She'd done it! She'd let him catch her...which meant she trusted him. Knox felt a wobbly smile overtake him.

Savannah's laughing gaze met his. "Ask me that again."

"W-will you ever trust me?"

She arched up and kissed him hungrily. She might as well have hot-wired his groin, for the effect Knox felt. "Baby, you can bet your sweet ass."

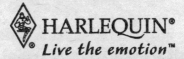

If you enjoyed what you just read,
then we've got an offer you can't resist!

Take 2 bestselling love stories FREE!

Plus get a FREE surprise gift!

Clip this page and mail it to Harlequin Reader Service®

IN U.S.A.
3010 Walden Ave.
P.O. Box 1867
Buffalo, N.Y. 14240-1867

IN CANADA
P.O. Box 609
Fort Erie, Ontario
L2A 5X3

YES! Please send me 2 free Blaze™ novels and my free surprise gift. After receiving them, if I don't wish to receive anymore, I can return the shipping statement marked cancel. If I don't cancel, I will receive 4 brand-new novels each month, before they're available in stores! In the U.S.A., bill me at the bargain price of $3.80 plus 25¢ shipping and handling per book and applicable sales tax, if any*. In Canada, bill me at the bargain price of $4.21 plus 25¢ shipping and handling per book and applicable taxes**. That's the complete price and a savings of at least 10% off the cover prices—what a great deal! I understand that accepting the 2 free books and gift places me under no obligation ever to buy any books. I can always return a shipment and cancel at any time. Even if I never buy another book from Harlequin, the 2 free books and gift are mine to keep forever.

150 HDN DNWD
350 HDN DNWE

Name	(PLEASE PRINT)	
Address	Apt.#	
City	State/Prov.	Zip/Postal Code

* Terms and prices subject to change without notice. Sales tax applicable in N.Y.
** Canadian residents will be charged applicable provincial taxes and GST.
All orders subject to approval. Offer limited to one per household and not valid to current Blaze™ subscribers.
® are registered trademarks of Harlequin Enterprises Limited.

BLZ02-R

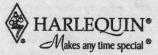

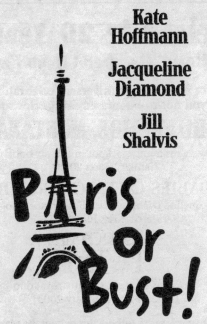

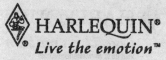

HARLEQUIN®
Temptation.

AMERICAN HEROES
These men are heroes—
strong, fearless...
And impossible to resist!

Join bestselling authors Lori Foster, Donna Kauffman
and Jill Shalvis as they deliver up

MEN OF COURAGE

Harlequin anthology
May 2003

Followed by *American Heroes* miniseries
in Harlequin Temptation

RILEY by Lori Foster
June 2003

SEAN by Donna Kauffman
July 2003

LUKE by Jill Shalvis
August 2003

Don't miss this sexy new miniseries by some of
Temptation's hottest authors!

Available at your favorite retail outlet.

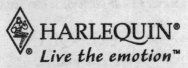

HARLEQUIN®
Live the emotion™

Visit us at www.eHarlequin.com

HTAH